177

BLIZZARD JUSTICE

After frostbite crippled the fingers of his gun hand, Isaac Morgan thought his days of chasing desperadoes were over. But when steel-hearted Deputy US Marshal Ambrose Bishop rides into town one winter evening, aiming to bait a trap for a brutal gang which has been terrorizing the border, Morgan's peace is shattered. For after the lawman's scheme misfires, and the miscreants snatch the town judge's beautiful daughter Kitty, Bishop and Morgan must join forces to get her back.

RANDOLPH VINCENT

BLIZZARD JUSTICE

Complete and Unabridged

LINFORD
Leicester

First published in Great Britain in 2014 by
Robert Hale Limited
London

First Linford Edition
published 2017
by arrangement with
Robert Hale
an imprint of
The Crowood Press
Wiltshire

A catalogue record for this book is available
from the British Library.

ISBN 978–1–4448–3381–2

Published by
F. A. Thorpe (Publishing)
Anstey, Leicestershire

Set by Words & Graphics Ltd.
Anstey, Leicestershire
Printed and bound in Great Britain by
T. J. International Ltd., Padstow, Cornwall

This book is printed on acid-free paper

1

Emile Beauclaire had been playing piano at The Dutchman's for as long as any of the saloon's regulars could remember. A sawed-off man with a spangled waistcoat stretched across a pot-belly, he started playing at three o'clock in the afternoon and finished twelve hours later. Every day he played the same tunes in the same order. In Lone Pine they said you could set your clock by Beau's piano. At that moment he was midway through *Turkey In The Straw*. Morgan reckoned that made it a few minutes after seven. He made note of the time because at that moment the stranger at the bar turned around.

Morgan was sitting in The Dutchman's drinking strong, black coffee and trying to untangle the intricacies of *Blackstone's Legal Commentaries* when the stranger walked into the saloon, politely asked

Muldoon the barkeep for a whiskey glass and the bottle to partner it, then set about drinking like he was mortal thirsty, running short on time, or both.

That had been forty-five minutes earlier — in the middle of *Strawberry Roan*. The Dutchman's was quiet at that point of the evening. A few cowpokes had ridden in from the Hampton place and were stoking up on beer and bourbon. Felix, the faro dealer, was trying to stir some bets from a couple of fancy-looking salesmen who'd arrived on the afternoon mud wagon. A group of old-timers sat in the corner, beneath a large portrait of an elegant lady, the significance of whom nobody — not even The Dutchman himself — could remember, discussing the Seventh Cavalry, expected presently to administer justice to the Indians, while at the angle of the bar, Jonas B Whitehead, proprietor, editor and chief reporter of the *Lone Pine Clarion*, searched for a front page story at the bottom of his brandy glass.

Those first few jolts of whiskey relaxed the stranger. His shoulders sank slightly and his drinking settled to a more leisurely pace. He was a little below six feet tall, aged around forty, with the rangy toughness of a ponderosa pine. From the crown of his black Mosby hat to the tips of his dark leather boots he was dusted from a long ride. His lean, angular face was speckled with smuts of dirt, his dark moustache and eyebrows powdered pale as prairie sand.

There was only one small corner of the stranger's appearance that didn't carry evidence of a hard journey and that was the Army Remington holstered on his right hip. The rosewood butt was burnished and the steel gleamed like cut crystal beneath the kerosene lamps of the saloon. Morgan had kept a keen eye on the stranger ever since that pistol caught his attention. Experience had taught him that any man who paid so little attention to his own cleanliness and so much to that of his sidearm needed watching.

So Morgan carefully eyed the stranger, observing the way he nonchalantly surveyed the saloon through the wide mirror that hung at the back of the bar, taking in the position of all those who sat in it, noting any iron they were carrying and weighing up what their faces said about how quick they'd be to use it.

It was the way Morgan himself would have done it back in Abilene, in the days before the Government tamed the place, when gunshots rattled out as regular as notes from the Frenchman's piano. Back then the only rule that existed was the one a man held in his heart and his hand. Working for the US Marshal Service, Morgan, fast, cool and fearless, had served as prosecutor or defender in more gun law cases than he cared to recall. The fact that he was still alive was evidence he'd won all of them.

Then came the Big White Out of '74. Morgan was on the prairie leading a posse in pursuit of a gang of renegades who'd ambushed and killed a family of settlers, when the fiercest snowstorm in living memory hit Kansas. Visibility dropped to a few feet, movement was impossible, and moisture froze in eyes and nostrils. Livestock died upright where it stood. Separated from the rest of the men, Morgan spent nigh on three days battling for life, hunkered leeside of his frozen mare. He made it through, but nature took her price: three toes on his left foot, fingers on both hands gnarled as cotton-oak roots and a shiver that could run down his spine even at noon on the hottest day of a summer.

Now Morgan felt that chill tingling in him again as he watched the stranger turn. The man moved with calm easiness, leant back on the bar, elbows wide, fingers tucked into his belt.

'Would you consider a request?' he called to Beau in a voice smooth as maple syrup.

The pianist stopped and turned to face his questioner, an ingratiating grin twitching between his trim moustache and clipped goatee.

'Of course, Monsieur, if I am familiar with the tune.'

The stranger smiled back at him. 'The one I'm hankering after is entitled 'Silence', or, to use a more colloquial name, 'Quit Jangling, Old Man, Or I'll Put A Hole In Your Head'.' He delivered these words evenly; then, smiling still, 'Is that part of your repertoire, *monsieur?*'

The Frenchman's rotund face flushed crimson. 'I-I-I ah-er, *m-m-monsieur* . . . .' he stammered.

'Would you like me to teach it you?' the stranger asked in a voice rich with cordiality.

Morgan closed the heavy legal tome he'd been studying. 'That won't be necessary, mister,' he said. His voice was quiet, but there was a flinty quality to it that cut through the hubbub of even the noisiest bar rooms. By now The Dutchman's was near silent as the patrons craned around to watch what looked like it might turn into an entertaining floorshow.

6

The stranger moved his head slowly to appraise Morgan. If he was ruffled by the intervention it did not show. He appeared at ease with the world, like a well-rested man surveying a fine sunrise over a plate of hot biscuits and bacon.

'Well now,' he said in the same slow, amiable tone with which he had menaced the pianist, 'I took a considered look at you when first I entered this hostelry, sir. Initial conclusion: that of all the rascals and ne'er-do-wells in here you were indubitably the one of the highest calibre. On closer inspection, however, I discovered that you are not all that you appear. More accurately: that you are a man of distinct parts. While you unquestionably have the eyes of a gunfighter,' he gestured with his head towards the table in front of Morgan, 'you also possess the hands of . . . a scarecrow.'

Morgan looked down at his knotted fingers, shook his head sadly as if in resignation, then lifted his hands up from the table and made a gesture like a man shooting the cuffs of his shirt. A split second later the stranger found himself looking at the business end of a six-barrelled 07-gauge pepperbox pistol.

The stranger's smile barely flickered. 'Ingeniously done, sir, ingeniously done,' he responded smoothly and with apparent admiration. 'I've seen a sleeve hold-out used to pop an ace into a cardsharp's hand, never a gun.

'But, you know,' the stranger continued, 'the critics say those derringers are very unreliable. Common opinion is you couldn't hit a bull buffalo with one at five paces, and even if you did the slugs would bounce off his hide like a handful of dried peas.'

'That what they say?' Morgan replied, his voice now a whisper, the third finger on his right hand — the only one he could rely on — gradually increasing the pressure on the pistol's unguarded trigger.

'By all accounts, yes,' the stranger said, cordial as before.

'You want to put that theory to the

test, make your move,' Morgan hissed.

The stranger looked him over slowly, taking in the grey-blue eyes and the grim set of the mouth and jaw, then moved his head gently to look at Beau.

'It appears I'm going to have to listen to you wrestling with that pianoforte whether I like it or not, *monsieur*,' he said, and without so much as a glance at Morgan he turned smoothly back to the bar and poured himself another drink.

The pianist looked at the back of the stranger, then at Morgan, searching for reassurance that the danger had passed. Morgan nodded to him that it had. Emile Beauclaire spun on his piano stool, took a deep breath, flexed his delicate fingers and began to play again.

Two minutes later the chatter of the saloon had recommenced, the recent drama was fading into legend and any regular walking through the swing doors of The Dutchman's would have known from the sound of Shenandoah that it was ten minutes after seven.

* ★ *

There was a sharp wintry chill on Lone Pine's main drag, and the scent of wood smoke in the air when Morgan stepped out of The Dutchman's. He looked up at a full moon which hung in the clear sky surrounded by a pool of light the colour of melted butter. He shivered, pulled his coat tighter around him and set off for Judge Persimmon's house and his nightly lesson in jurisprudence. The cold air tweaked Morgan's joints as he stepped along the boardwalk. The missing toes on his left foot didn't affect walking, but if he attempted any speed above a slow trot he was likely to topple over like a toddler. Seeing Morgan ruled out from being a lawman any more, Judge Persimmon had persuaded the young man to become a lawyer instead.

'During your time as an officer of my court you struck me as a young man who clearly knows the difference between right and wrong,' the white-haired Persimmon had remarked with a cynical chuckle. 'Now it's time to forget all about that and concentrate on the law!'

As he strode along, hunched against the frosty night, Morgan noticed Plug Watson — seventeen-year-old son of the town's sheriff, Deke Watson — standing out on the steps of the town jail looking cold and anxious.

'What you about tonight, Plug?' Morgan asked as he drew alongside.

Watson flushed, 'My daddy deputized me, Mr Morgan,' he replied, stepping from one foot to the other like a man eagerly awaiting his turn in the water closet. 'We got us a prisoner, see. Real bad man from up in the Black Hills.'

'Your father arrested an outlaw?' Morgan said, struggling to keep the note of surprise out of his voice. Sheriff Watson was a portly, amiable fellow, and more noted for his ability to eat pie than apprehend villains.

'N-n-nope,' Plug stammered, pulling a Colt pistol out of the holster at his hip and cocking and uncocking it nervously.

'US marshal brung him in 'bout an hour since.'

Morgan watched the boy fiddling with the firing mechanism of the revolver. The gun was bright and shiny, not because it was well looked after, as the stranger's weapon had been, but because it was brand new — broken out of the sheriff's office gun case a few minutes ago, no doubt.

'You best stop twiddling with the hammer on that pistol,' Morgan said. 'Way you're carrying on, the darn thing's likely to go off and hurt somebody.'

Plug twitched. 'Yep, sir, I s'pose,' he said, and reholstered the gun. 'Guess I'm just kinda nervous on account of this outlaw we got.'

You were born nervous, Morgan thought, but he kept it to himself. 'Marshal brought him in, huh?' he asked.

Plug blushed again, unused to the attention. 'Sure did, Mr Morgan. Slung across the back of his horse, knocked cold.'

'The marshal inside with your pa?'

Morgan enquired, nodding towards the office door.

'No, he ain't,' Plug said. 'Daddy's guarding the varmint solo and I'm posted lookout. Marshal took his bags across to Sullivan's Hotel, then headed on to The Dutchman's. Tall fella in one of them round-topped Reb Cavalry hats. You see him when you was in there?'

Morgan smiled ruefully as he recalled his encounter with the stranger in the Mosby hat.

'And fully made the man's acquaintance too,' he said. 'You catch his name, Plug?'

'Certainly did,' the youngster replied. There was a pause.

'You like to share it with me?' Morgan said eventually.

'Sure,' Plug responded. 'It was, er, erm . . . sorry, Mr Morgan, all this excitement's gotten my head in a spin. It was, let me think . . . a church name. Priest? No, that wasn't it, Pope?'

'Bishop?' Morgan said.

Plug grinned, enthusiastically nodding his head 'That's it, Mr Morgan. You know him?'

'Know of him,' Morgan said. And, leaving aside hermits and half-wit boys, who didn't? Deputy US Marshal Ambrose Bishop was the most feared lawman in the North-West territories.

'Certainly seemed a very polite gentleman,' Plug said, removing the gun from its holster again, then quickly sliding it back when Morgan glared at him.

'Did the marshal say what this scamp he brought in was wanted for?' Morgan enquired.

Plug shrugged. 'Shot a fella,' he answered, attempting to sound casual about it.

'Whereabouts?' Morgan asked.

Plug Watson reddened again. 'In . . . in the backside, Mr Morgan,' he said.

Morgan let out an exasperated sigh and shook his head. 'Whereabouts in the *Territory?*' he enquired.

The youngster twitched. 'Oh, right. I thought you meant, well . . . Yankton, I guess it was.'

Morgan thought about it for a moment. Why bring the outlaw here? Why not take him back to where the crime was committed? It seemed a curious decision, but doubtless Bishop had his reasons. The marshal was the calculating type. Morgan had seen that in The Dutchman's. Even when he'd had the drop on Bishop, it appeared the man was tallying the odds, until — like a seasoned gambler — he'd decided the pot wasn't big enough to make it worth while calling his opponent's bluff. Other men wouldn't have backed down. Their pride wouldn't have allowed it. But Bishop approached his trade like a professional poker player. He never made things personal. He based his decisions on percentages, never on feelings.

Morgan looked at Plug, who was back fiddling with the butt of the pistol. If he could get through the night without blowing a hole in his foot it would be a miracle. No benefit in undermining the boy's confidence, though, so he smiled encouragingly at him instead.

'Well, with you and your daddy mastering the situation I think the town can rest easy. G'night, Plug,' and with a tip of his Stetson Morgan set off down the street.

2

Bishop's given name was Ambrose, though it was hard to imagine that anyone, even his own mother, had ever called him by it. On account of his surname, courteous manner and fancy diction enemies called him the Clergyman. And Bishop had many enemies. Happily for him most of them were in jail, or the grave. He knew, because he had put them there. It was his job, or part of it at least.

In the sprawling wilderness of the Dakota Territory Bishop was tasked with administering justice, taking census and proclaiming edicts issued 1,300 miles away in Washington DC. Wherever Bishop stood the silver badge he wore pinned on the inside of his coat lapel declared that not only was he the law, he was the government too.

The outlaw whom Bishop had

dropped into the jail was named Billy Bearpaw. Bearpaw was a young miscreant with a long list of offences to his name. Petty stuff mainly: drunkenness, property damage, and a failed attempt to scalp an undertaker in Sioux Falls. Most recently he'd discharged a sawn-off shotgun through the window of a draper's store in Yankton, leaving the draper with a backside like a colander. He'd live, but he'd not sit down much before Easter, and it was currently two months shy of Christmas.

Following the drapery incident Bearpaw and his longtime associate Frank Petty had made a run for the Black Hills. The boys were howling drunk, their horses were raw, and Bishop had caught up with them inside of six hours. He could have apprehended both, but that wouldn't have suited his purpose, so he let Petty slip away and homed in on Bearpaw.

The youngster was not much use with a rifle and no better with a sidearm. His main method of self-defence, as far as Bishop could judge, was yelling, long, hard and continually in a voice a little too high-pitched to be tolerable. The volume was reduced substantially when his captor struck Bearpaw a blow above the ear with the barrel of his pistol. After that Bishop had folded the tethered miscreant over the saddle of his pony and ridden on to Lone Pine, pausing every dozen miles to remind his prisoner to keep the noise down.

By the time he dumped Bearpaw at the town jail the youngster had concussion and Bishop had a jangling headache, which the sound of Frenchie's keyboard had irritated badly. As Bishop admitted defeat to the crooked fingered fellow with the pepperbox pistol in The Dutchman's and turned his attention back to his whiskey he pondered on the fact that a combination of a boy's bawling and an out of tune piano had come as close to getting him killed as the gunplay of two dozen bandits.

Bishop poured himself another measure and sipped it quietly. His peace was short-lived.

'You act pretty tough with pi'nists n' cripples, mister,' a voice behind him said. 'How you like t' throw down with a *real* man?'

Bishop looked up at the long mirror behind the bar. The man with the pepperbox pistol had quit the place ten minutes before, leaving the saloon empty of anyone likely to disturb his equilibrium. Sure enough, the speaker was the leader of the cowhands, a rat-faced man he'd swiftly marked down as a bitter little blowhard. He'd plainly been hitting the bottle. His cheeks were the colour of his red bandanna, his brow was glistening with sweat beneath a greasy mop of dark locks, and there were flecks of saliva in the stubble around his lips.

'Y' hear me?' the man snarled, struggling to keep the slur out of his voice.

Bishop turned with his habitual leisureliness. He looked at the speaker with the same benevolent smile with which he'd surveyed Morgan's gun barrels.

'What y' gotta say for yourself, mister?' the man growled again, spittle flying. His hands, Bishop noted, were poised three inches above a pair of holstered Colts. Odd, he thought, how often it is that men who can't handle a single gun insist on waving two at you.

'I think,' Bishop said in his calm, even tone, 'that you, sir, are an inebriate.'

The drunk scowled angrily. 'No I ain't,' he spat. 'I'm an 'Merican just like you is. More so, pr'aly, you, you, you . . .'

As the drunkard struggled to find a suitable insult, Bishop's eyes slid to the left as if to glance at something coming up from the rear. Catching the look the rat-faced man jerked his head around.

The split second this action gave Bishop was all he needed. The marshal took one long stride forward, drawing his Remington as he did so and spinning it on his trigger finger. As the drunk — satisfied now that he was not about to be bushwhacked from behind — swung back to look at the lawman, his jaw ran straight into the swinging butt-end of the revolver.

The cattleman crashed to the floor, out cold. His three workmates who had been observing the scene rose groggily to their feet, fingers poised above pistols. Bishop smiled politely at them.

'You gentlemen use your hands to grab a hold of anything more than fresh air and you'll be dead before you hit the deck,' he said as calmly as a waiter announcing that dinner was served, 'You have my word on that.'

The cowhands looked at Bishop, at their colleague unconscious at his feet, and at the revolver that was now — as if by some magical sleight of hand — back in its holster. They were drunk, but they weren't stupid. Not that stupid anyway. Their shoulders slumped and their hands dropped to their sides in surrender.

'Be good enough to take him with you when you leave, won't you?' Bishop said before turning back to the bar and signalling to Muldoon for his tab.

Morgan stepped up on to the porch of Judge Persimmon's home — a two-storey white clapboard house that looked as if it might have been transported from the owner's native Virginia — and, bunching his fingers into as near as they would come to a fist, rapped on the glass-panelled front door.

'Come on in, Mr Morgan,' a mellow female voice called out.

On hearing it Morgan wrestled down two conflicting urges: the first to turn and run away, the second to whoop with delight. He did neither, instead removing his hat and inexpertly smoothing down his sandy-red hair with one crooked hand, before opening the door and stepping inside.

Kitty Persimmon, the judge's daughter, was standing in the circular hallway, a cut-glass vase of dried lavender flowers in her hand. She was dressed in a Prussian-blue silk skirt, a crisp white blouse and a black Spanish shawl. The blouse was pinned at the throat with a brooch of lapis lazuli that matched her eyes. Her golden hair was worn up in a chignon. Local gossip said she'd been engaged to a young Confederate officer killed at Gettysburg, and thereafter had vowed never to marry. Morgan had no idea if that were true, and was too afraid to ask her in case he found that it was.

As he entered the house Kitty smiled and dimples appeared in her cheeks. Despite himself Morgan felt an idiot grin spreading across his face.

'Evening, Miss Persimmon,' he said, twiddling the hat in his gnarled fist and feeling suddenly as foolish as 'Plug' Watson.

'You appear in good humour, Mr Morgan,' Kitty replied, cocking her head and studying him with what appeared — to him at least — to be amusement. 'Is it the prospect of several hours listening to my father recount his experiences of the court-house, or has something occurred that tickled you?'

'Well,' Morgan said, 'I just discovered that Sheriff Watson has deputized his son and the pair of them are currently standing guard over some young desperado at the town jail.'

'Are you insinuating,' Kitty said, 'that the combined forces of the Watson menfolk are insufficient for the task?'

'I'm suggesting,' Morgan responded, 'that if brains were gunpowder neither of them would have enough to blow his hat off.'

To his delight Kitty laughed, her blue eyes sparkling, then she said in a mock-stern voice, 'Really, Mr Morgan, you should know better than to poke fun at the institutions of the law, especially in this house.'

'That you, Isaac?' the judge's gruff Southern-accented voice boomed from behind the door of his study.

'The master calls,' Kitty said with a smile. 'Would you like me to bring you some coffee?'

'Thank you, I've had plenty already,' Morgan said, then cursed himself for throwing away another chance to see Kitty, then cursed himself again for thinking that any woman so lovely might want anything to do with him.

'Well, in that case I'll bid you good night, Mr Morgan.' With a nod she walked off down the corridor to the kitchen. After a few yards, she turned and looked back at him. Briefly their eyes met and Morgan felt a jolt like he'd been kicked in the forehead by a mule.

Then she was gone. He took a couple of deep breaths, steadied himself and ten minutes later was inhaling the smoke of the judge's cigar and immersing himself in torts and precedents.

★ ★ ★

Sheriff Watson was by no means as tubby as Lone Pine folk tended to make out, but certainly nobody was ever going to mistake him for a garden rake. He was five feet eight and his belly rested on his belt like a sack of oats balanced on a fence rail. Shortly after Morgan had had his conversation with Deputy Watson his father emerged from his office and said he was feeling dizzy with thirst and hunger and needed to make an emergency visit to The Dutchman's for a ham hock and a glass of cold Dortmunder beer. He handed his son the keys, told him to go inside, lock the door after him and not open it again to anybody but himself and the marshal.

Plug had done as he was told and now sat uneasily at his father's desk, fighting the urge to put his feet up on it. The sheriff's office was a square room containing the desk and some chairs. There was a gun rack behind the desk, lined with shotguns and Winchester repeating rifles, the ammunition for which was in the drawer of the desk. A cast-iron stove kept the place warm, heated up the coffee and fried the bacon and pancakes that the officer of the law liked to have for breakfast. The single, steel-barred jail cell was in the corner of the room furthest from the door. Eight feet square, it contained a cot and a chamberpot. Mindful of the potential for mischief, the builders had not given it a window.

Plug jiggled the keys absent-mindedly in his hand and imagined himself a lawman like his daddy or, better still, Deputy US Marshal Bishop, when he heard the prisoner come back to consciousness with a groan.

In the cell Billy Bearpaw rubbed the side of his throbbing head and struggled to get his eyes to focus. He remembered being taken by the marshal and hit over the head, but beyond that everything was kind of dark and blurred.

'You feeling all right, mister?' Plug Watson asked nervously, getting to his feet and walking towards the cell. He stopped five feet from the bars, scared to go any closer. This was a real-life badman, after all.

Billy rose groggily to his feet. He was small, shorter than Plug and wirily built. His hair was jet black, his skin was dark as hardwood. He smelled of woodsmoke, sweat and stale beer. Bearpaw's eyes were close set and one slid slightly inwards, giving his face a look of menacing stupidity.

'You got any whiskey?' he asked.

'No sir,' Plug said.

'You going to let me out so I can go get some?' the outlaw asked. He grinned at Plug, but there was nothing friendly in it.

'Can't do that,' the young deputy said. 'The marshal as brung you in wouldn't like it.'

Billy Bearpaw spat on the floor, then stared at Plug. 'If I was you,' he said, 'I'd be a lot less scared of what *might* happen if you *do* let me out, than I would of what *will* happen if you *don't*.'

'How d'you figure that, mister?' Plug asked nervously.

Bearpaw scratched himself thoughtfully, enjoying the fear in the other boy's face.

'Well, see my friend Frank he escaped from that marshal. And Frank will have gone and told my uncle that I got buffaloed by a yellow-bellied Yankee and now I'm locked in a jail cell in . . . ?

'Lone Pine,' Plug said, then wondered if he should have kept it secret.

' . . . Lone Pine,' Bearpaw repeated with a nod. 'And when my uncle hears that he's going to be mighty angry. He's going to come and bust me out. He'll kill anyone tries to stop him.'

'Sure,' Plug responded trying to sound tough. 'You say.'

Billy Bearpaw cocked his head to one side and narrowed his eyes, putting his best gunslinger stare on the deputy.

'My uncle,' he said, lowering his voice, 'he's slain many, many people. Men, women, children; don't matter to him just so long as they're white. See, my uncle he hates white people. And you, boy, you're as white as buttermilk. He's gonna slit your throat and scalp you, for sure. And if he does it quick, then you just be real grateful. You understand?'

Plug stared at Billy Bearpaw for a

moment his mind filled with the lurid overheard conversations about Indian atrocities that his momma always avoided. Eventually he shook his head, took a deep breath and in the coolest voice he could muster said:

'I believe you're all talk, mister. I bet you ain't even got an uncle.' He turned away and went back to his Daddy's desk. He opened the Lone Pine Clarion and tried to read it, but he couldn't concentrate on the newspaper stories for the gory imaginings running through his head.

★ ★ ★

Deputy US Marshal Ambrose Bishop entered the cramped foyer of Sullivan's Hotel. It was stained the colour of nicotine, contained a battered reception desk, two sagging leather armchairs and a stuffed Kodiac bear. The bear was rearing up on its hind legs, in all likelihood in protest at the filthiness of the carpet. The proprietor, Headley

Sullivan, a ginger-haired, red-faced man, was sitting behind the desk, head buried the *Lone Pine Clarion*.

'What can I get you?' the hotelier snapped, finally rising from his chair, having pointedly ignored Bishop for as long as it took to study the classified advertisements.

'I called in an hour ago and reserved a room for the next three nights,' Bishop said in his characteristically even tone. 'That valise is mine,' he added, indicating a yellow leather case propped up against the wall behind the desk.

Headley Sullivan spat vermilion tobacco juice in the general direction of a filthy brass spittoon nestling at the feet of the bear. He snatched a key from the rack behind him and slapped it on the desk.

'Room four, back of the building, overlooking the muleskinner's yard. Breakfast's included in the price, but the kitchen closes at 8 a.m. sharp. If you turn up thirty seconds late you'll go hungry.'

He moved to go back to his chair, but Bishop raised a hand. 'I did request a

32

room at the front,' he said mildly.

'Well, so you did, mister,' Sullivan said with a scowl, 'But your luck is out, 'cause two fancy-pants snake-oil salesmen from Chicago just moved into that one.'

Bishop sighed and rubbed the bridge of his nose. 'Would you object if I were to approach them and ask them to swap,' he asked.

'What you do with your time is your own damn fool business,' Sullivan retorted. 'But don't expect me to come up there moving bags and changing linen for you.'

Bishop looked into the sour, piggy eyes of the hotelier, felt rage rising in him and choked it back. He didn't want to draw attention to himself. The fewer people who knew he was in Lone Pine the better. He'd already involved himself in one scrimmage and come close to another. Instead of pistol-whipping his ill-mannered host, he contented himself with smiling affably and remarking, 'Your magnanimity, sir, is exceeded only by your graciousness.'

Sullivan stared nastily at him. 'You've certainly got a mouth full of five dollar words, mister,' he said, spat once again on to the carpet and stalked off into the office behind the reception desk, slamming the door behind him.

Bishop took the key from the desk and put it in his pocket, picked up his case and ascended the stairs. The room that overlooked the street was number three. A sound of laughter came from within. He knocked and a few moments later the door was flung open by a tall, skinny, auburn-haired man in a wide-collared cream shirt and plaid pants held up by red braces.

'Good evening, good sir,' the tall man said with theatrical enthusiasm, looking Bishop up and down. 'Holbrooke Wade, travelling representative at your service. The hour is late, yet I hazard that news of the quality of our wares has already permeated the hostelries and domestic domiciles of this remarkable conurbation. I judge from your appearance, sir that you are a man who savours the very finest things this life has to offer. Perhaps therefore I can interest you in our range of Lasseter and Tweed toiletries?'

Bishop felt his headache stirring again. 'I am a Deputy US marshal and require this room for matters of legal business,' he said, managing a placatory grin despite his irritation. 'There is another identical one across the landing. I will help you move your bags.'

With a brief apology he brushed past Wade and into the room. The second travelling salesman was lying on the double bed with his boots off and his striped satin waistcoat unbuttoned. His blue-black hair was parted in the middle, his moustache waxed and elaborately curled.

'My dear sir . . . ' he warbled in protest as Bishop placed his stiff leather case down on a circular table at the foot of the bed.

The room smelled heavily of cheroot smoke, cheap cologne and creeping damp; the cream wallpaper was mottled with mildew, the varnished pine floor speckled with burn marks. A tinted, fly-blown print depicting Andrew Jackson's victory at New Orleans hung on the far wall, opposite it a tall sash window looked straight across to the town jail. Bishop strode across the room and opened the window.

'I say, the night is chill!' the salesman named Wade said, following him to the window. 'And my colleague, Mr Rathbone, suffers from a weakening of the chest. May I ask what the devil this is about?'

Bishop did not respond. Instead he took a brief survey of the view from the window, then walked back to the table, popped the catches on his case and lifted the lid. Inside were a marksman's steel tripod and an octagonal-barrelled Sharps buffalo rifle. Bishop picked them up and returned to the window, Wade trailing behind him, sputtering in complaint, while his colleague Rathbone added to the chorus of disapproval from the bed.

Bishop set up the tripod in front of the window, knelt down, placed the barrel of the rifle on the rest, flipped up the circular rear sight and looked through it. The Sharps was a single shot breech-loader. It was of little use in a close quarters scrap against a foe with a rapid firing gun such as a Winchester or a Colt, but at long range, in the hands of an expert, it was the deadliest gun in America. Not that total accuracy was essential. The buffalo rifle fired a high-calibre hollow-point bullet that would blow a hole in a man so big a jackrabbit could live in it. Any wound from it was likely to be fatal.

'I ask you once more, sir: what you are about?' Wade yelped. The marshal lifted the barrel of the rifle from the stand and, still kneeling with the weapon snug to his shoulder, turned slowly round.

'Forgive my rudeness,' he replied moderately, 'but I dislike people watching over me when I'm working. It makes me . . . ' he paused, staring at the open throat of Wade's shirt through the circular gunsight, ' . . . edgy.'

He dug in his pocket with his left hand, fished out the key Sullivan had given him and tossed it to Wade. 'Room four, across the hall,' he said. 'I believe you'll be very comfortable there.'

'We leave,' the salesman named Rathbone huffed, 'though not without registering our protest. And, I must add, sir, that a gentleman with a moustache as thick and lustrous as your own would surely benefit from the purchase of some of Lasseter and Tweeds illustrious waxing unguent — redolent of Parisian nights, yet . . . '

He stopped as he saw Bishop swing the gun from his colleague to himself, the muzzle level with his belly button. 'Ah, but I sense that perhaps now is not the time. I leave a catalogue and a complimentary application on the cabinet for consideration at your leisure. We shall be here till Thursday noon, prices negotiable, discounts for bulk purchases.' He rose from the bed and began hastily bundling samples and clothing into a carpetbag.

Bishop returned to the window and continued his appraisal of the jail where Billy Bearpaw was being guarded by the fat sheriff and his idiot son. A minute or so later he heard the door of the room close behind him.

* * *

'Marshal Ambrose Bishop, you say?' Judge Persimmon murmured, swirling the golden Kentucky bourbon round in his glass, breathing in the vanilla scent of the oak casks it had matured in. 'Now, there is a name with which to conjure.'

The law lesson was over and Morgan and his teacher were now mulling over the news of the day with the help of some of Persimmon's finest Southern sipping-whiskey.

'You've met him?' Morgan asked.

'Oh yes,' the old judge replied with a nod. 'A number of times in Dodge,

Abilene and Helena. He is one of those enforcers — Earp and Masterson are others — who remain just a whisker on our side of the law. As the Duke of Wellington remarked of his troops, 'I don't know what they do to the enemy, but by God they frighten me!'' The judge chuckled at the great general's witticism. 'Rough men, Isaac. But this is a rough place.'

'I guess I might have been one of them, if . . . ' Morgan's voice trailed away as he raised one of his gnarled hands.

The judge smiled at him. 'I don't think so, my boy. You were quick enough with a gun, certainly, but you lack the implacable ruthlessness of men like Bishop.' Seeing a faint look of dismay appear on Morgan's face, he added, 'Human decency is nothing to be ashamed of, Isaac. I meant what I just said as a compliment.'

Morgan nodded. 'Yet Bishop seemed very polite, well-mannered — amiable even.'

The judge smiled. 'In my experience that is often the way with his type. I recall some time back spending a pleasant hour in conversation with a certain Captain Jack Slade. He was the very soul of affability and consideration. Six months later I read that this same Slade had lashed a horse thief to a fence, shot him twenty-two times and sliced off his ears. They say he killed two dozen men in total, yet you could not have encountered a fellow more courteous, or more likely to charm your dear old mother. It is my belief that such men do not waste a single ounce of nastiness unnecessarily, but save it all up for the moment when they need it most.'

The judge glanced up at the oak-cased Georgian grandfather clock that had accompanied his ancestors from England and had pride of place in the corner of his book-lined study. 'Ah, but Isaac, it is nearly eleven o'clock,' he remarked. 'You had better get across to the Widow Jennings' boarding house before she locks up for the night and you are forced to sleep in the stable with the mules.'

The judge accompanied Morgan to the door. 'You know what happened to Jack Slade?' he asked as they stood together on the porch. Morgan said he didn't. 'Forgot his manners up in Montana and some vigilantes hanged him,' the judge said. 'They say his wife had him buried in a zinc coffin filled with whiskey.' He gave a wheezing chuckle, then his face became solemn. 'Fate lies in wait for men like that. You mark it, Isaac,' he said and with a nod sent the younger man off into the freezing night.

*　*　*

At that same moment Bishop had begun to nod off in the moth-eaten armchair he'd positioned by the window of his room. In the years he'd spent in his job he'd tackled some of the worst outlaws the territory had spewed up: heartless men who killed for money, or fun, or both. Even compared to the nicest of them, Bearpaw was spit in the wind. The marshal hadn't hunted the youngster down for the crimes he'd committed. He'd hunted him down because of who he was.

For more than five years a loose-knit clan of badmen who operated from inside the wooded, Sioux-infested fastness of the Black Hills had plagued the Dakota Territory. The gang had ambushed wagon trains, burned home-steads, terrorized townships. At least fifty slayings were credited to them. Man, woman, or child, it made no difference.

The gang's leader was a scar-faced woodsman, a Metis whose people had fought the British in Canada for nigh on a century. His name was Louis Longeye. Billy Bearpaw was his favourite nephew.

Bishop had trailed Longeye and his gang more times than he liked to recall. He wasn't the only one: marshals, sheriffs and posses from all over the territory had chased him. So had the

Royal Canadian Mounted Police and the British Army. They had hunted him with White and Indian trackers and with dogs brought over especially from Ireland. But years of living in the backwoods as trapper and outlaw had made the Metis as wily as a mink. He knew the wild country better than any living creature, and every hideaway in it from cave to hollow log. He knew how to cover his tracks and leave false trails, when to run like the wind and when to stand still as a rock.

Sometimes Bishop had felt he was almost close enough to touch his prey, only to find that a moment later he'd gone again. The Indians, Bishop knew, thought that Longeye was a shape-shifter — a sorcerer who could change his form into that of another living creature, soaring away from his pursuers on the wings of an eagle, or hiding from them inside a turtle's shell. Bishop did not hold with such heathen superstition, yet there were times when even he found himself wondering if magic wasn't the only possible explanation for Longeye's ability to disappear like mist in the noonday sun.

Unable to find Longeye, Bishop had decided that he would let Longeye find him. By now Frank Petty would be halfway to the Black Hills to relay news of Bearpaw's capture to the gang leader. The gang would set off for Lone Pine at dawn, arriving in the late afternoon. They'd reconnoitre the jail, find it flimsily guarded, then wait until sunset to strike. Bishop would be waiting. The moon was full, the sky clear. Even at night it would be light enough for a crack shot to pick his target. All the marshal had to do was sit back, be patient, and wait.

3

It had snowed, but no more than a dusting, and the mule cart's wheels bumped freely across the frozen ground. There were two men in the cart, muffled in trade blankets against the cold of the high mountain meadow country. Both had beards. One was copper-coloured, the other fair. Watching them from his position amongst the trees Louis Longeye could not decide if they were Norwegians or Irish. As the cart came nearer fragments of their talk came skipping to him across the crisp white ground. He did not recognize the words. Perhaps it was German.

Longeye had seen the men first just after dawn. He spotted them through the brass telescope his grandfather had taken from a dead British officer and which had given his family its name. He had watched them for several hours, trundling gradually towards him and their journey's end. Wherever the men came from, they had travelled a long way to die.

Longeye's forefathers had travelled too, from France. They had lived by hunting and trapping, like the red men. Then the English came. The English brought their tame animals — cattle and pigs. They tried to tame the wild land so that their tame animals would be safe in it. Those who wanted to live in the old way were pushed west, and every time they found a place that was good the English — or the others who followed them — came and pushed them again. And again. And again.

Longeye's grandfather had moved. His father had moved. He had moved too. The last time here to the Black Hills. The Black Hills were the sacred land of the Sioux, the tribe of Longeye's grandmother (for the Sioux had also been driven west by the white men, out of their native forests and on to the grass prairies). He had come here last winter and resolved to go no further. Let the English and the other white men come. He would kill them as they killed the buffalo, remorselessly, relentlessly until the plains were pale with their bones.

The men in the cart were no more than a hundred paces from Longeye now. They knew that this was hostile country and they were watchful, yet they did not see him. His pale clothes and black-and-white face paint were carefully chosen. He was not hiding. Longeye did not hide. Standing stock still amongst the silver birches he just melted into the background of bright snow and dark, leafless branches.

When the cart was fifty paces off Longeye slowly and smoothly raised his long-barrelled Hawken hunting rifle. The weapon was darkened with a mix of bear fat and soot. There was no glint from the barrel to alert his prey.

Longeye waited, watching. He decided to shoot the one who spoke next. Seconds passed. The mule cart rolled forwards.

Then the man with the reddish beard opened his mouth. He was dead before he had uttered his second word.

The fair man watched his companion slump forwards and tumble from the cart. It was a moment before he realized what had happened. Then his eyes widened and his head twisted rapidly from side to side. When he saw the smoke from Longeye's gun he drew a pistol from beneath his blanket cloak, tugged on the brake of the wagon, jumped down and ducked away out of sight behind it.

Prevented from running, the mule-team stamped the ground and brayed fearfully. When the man was dead Longeye would send the women to bring the mules back to camp. He wished oxen had pulled the cart. The meat of mules was tough and acrid. But winter was here. He had twenty mouths to feed. He could not afford to be fussy.

Longeye moved a few paces to his right, away from the bitter blue mist left by the black powder. The Hawken was a flintlock muzzle-loader, but Longeye had carried one since childhood and the use of powder horn and ramrod was as easy and natural to him as walking. Crouching and tilting his head to one side he could see the fair-bearded man's feet on the other side of the cart. He lay down on the snow, sighted his rifle on the left boot.

Before he could pull the trigger another shot rang out and the fair-bearded man's entire body dropped into view, blood spreading from an exit wound in his chest. Longeye rose to his feet. Moments later a dark-skinned man with hair the colour of a silver fox's pelt, rifle slung over his shoulder, emerged from a cluster of aspens fifty paces beyond the cart. He was wearing a hooded coat made from a Hudson Bay blanket, red leather leggings and raccoonskin cap. Longeye raised his right hand in salute to the man, whose name was Jack Marat. Marat returned the gesture, and as he did so the steel blade of the scalping knife he held in his fist flashed in the sharp winter sun.

'Time was, *ami*,' Marat said later as they walked back up towards the camp, 'we'd have shot that last boy in the leg. Put him down, then spent a day or so finishing him off. Now,' he chuckled nastily, 'they coming so thick and fast we can't have no fun. I tell you, Louis, sometimes this killing feel more like a chore than a pleasure.' He spoke in French, but with such a nasal twang it is doubtful the inhabitants of Paris or Bordeaux would have understood a word he said.

'You tired of it, you move on,' Longeye said. He and Marat had been friends since boyhood. They had hunted and fought side by side for more than thirty years. They shared the same mixed heritage, but somehow in Marat the French side of it was stronger. Longeye was six feet four inches tall, with the wide, bulky shoulders of a bison, dark hair and eyes set in a wide expressionless face; Marat was a head shorter, silver-bearded, his blue-grey eyes twinkled, his movements were quick and agile. Longeye was silent by nature, his friend only by necessity. When the situation allowed talk, he talked. Longeye, as always, listened, though not always to Marat.

'We move any further, Louis, we going to fall in the sea,' Marat replied with a laugh. 'I'm not complaining, *copain*. Just observing, you know? The Lakota was supposed to have signed a treaty, give them the Black Hills for ever. No white men allowed in here by order of Washington. Then they find gold. Right here! Now these people they going to come and keep on coming. No amount of death going to deter them. And you and me, we got nowhere left to go. Louis, sometimes I think if it weren't for bad luck we'd have no luck at all.'

They came to the camp. It was situated high on a flat piece of land on the southern side of a high hill. To the north of it rose a steep cliff. From the ledges of the cliff a lookout could see for miles across the plains. It was from here that Longeye had spotted the mule-cart.

Pine trees surrounded the camp's remaining three sides and a river ran to the south of it providing fresh water. It was sheltered from the worst of the wind by the cliff and the trees, but there were still wide enough views to see any approaching strangers. The twenty people who lived at the camp — ten men, six women and four children — occupied a mix of buffalo-hide tepees and rough wooden cabins made of pine logs with roofs of branches, canvas and moss.

In the centre of the camp a fire burned and a smell of coffee wafted from a kettle. A dun pony was tethered to a ground peg near by, steam rising from its hot flanks.

'Young Frank's back,' Marat observed, gesturing towards it. 'But it don't look like your nephew's with him. Off chasing tail in town. Either that or he's gambled that chestnut mare of his away at some crap table and ridden back doubled up.'

Longeye looked at the dun pony. 'Whoever rode it came back real fast,' he said and he yelled for Frank.

A young man in a buckskin jacket and faded blue shirt emerged from one of the cabins. He was thin with shaggy black hair and the nervous manner of a dog that expects to be kicked.

'Sure glad to see you, Louis,' he said when he stood before Longeye and Marat. He spoke rapidly. 'Billy got took by a marshal, We was in Yankton. Billy shot a storekeeper spoke back to him. He weren't bad hurt, We run for it anyhow. The marshal come after us. 'Bout four hours out of Yankton he took Billy.'

When Frank Petty had finished Longeye gazed at him for what seemed to the youngster like a long, hard time. 'Billy's hurt?' he asked eventually.

'Not bad, I don't reckon,' Frank said. 'The marshal beat him some, but there weren't no shots.'

Longeye watched him while he spoke. 'How you know that?' he asked.

'I seen it happen,' Frank said, then wished he hadn't.

'You telling me,' Longeye said, 'you watched this marshal catch my nephew and beat him and you do nothing about it, just turn and run back here?'

'That ain't the way it was,' Frank replied, his voice rising with fear. 'I followed 'em. The marshal didn't know I was there. I trailed 'em to Lone Pine. That's where Billy is now. In the jail in Lone Pine.'

'You trailed him?' Longeye asked.

'Yes, Louis,' Frank said. 'To Lone Pine.'

'You didn't shoot this marshal that doesn't know you're there?'

'Look, see,' Frank replied, 'he had Billy slung across his horse. It was night. Maybe if I shot at him I'd hit Billy. It was dark. I was drunk. Honest, Louis, I done what I thought was right.'

'Run?' Longeye said.

'I only done it so as you'd know where he was. So we could go and rescue him. If the marshal had of got me too, well, nobody would've knowed where we was until it was too late.'

Longeye looked at him for a moment, then he turned and walked to his tepee, Marat followed him leaving Frank Petty standing by the campfire shivering, though it was not cold.

'You want me to kill that yellow pig?' Marat asked when they were inside. Longeye sat down on a buffalo rug. 'If I wanted him killed he'd be dead already,' he said. He did not speak again for nearly an hour.

When he did he said simply, 'Something is not right.'

*   *   *

Jack Marat rode into Lone Pine around noon. He was mounted on a strawberry roan pony. Behind him trailed one of the cart mules, a coffee brown molly he'd named Queen Victoria. 'That way,' he told his squaw, Two-Birds, 'I won't feel bad if I have to whip her.'

Queen Victoria was laden with prospecting kit taken from the men they'd killed the previous morning. Marat had taken off his regular woodsman's costume of buckskin jacket, leather leggings and moccasins, replacing it with a plaid shirt, wool trousers, and an Ulster of thick Donegal tweed some unfortunate Irish immigrant they'd encountered three weeks since wouldn't be needing any more. The braided side-locks of his long silver hair were tucked up under a brown derby hat. He looked like a typical gold-panner, riding in on his way to the Black Hills and willing to risk any danger for the glint of yellow amongst the gravel.

Marat tethered his horse and the mule to a hitching rail outside The Dutch-man's saloon. Compared to moccasins the boots were as heavy as lead and the rigid hide chafed his ankles. The wool shirt was itchy against his neck. Bridling against the strange clothes, he edged his way across the thoroughfare.

The town was busy at this hour with ox-drawn wagons, mule trains and groups of riders churning up the frosted earth that formed the surface of Main Street.

Marat nudged past a buckboard, dodged a small herd of sheep being driven into town by a donkey-mounted German settler and stepped up on to the boardwalk. Pausing briefly to tug at his shirt collar, he clumped along past the town jail.

There was a chubby, balding man standing in the doorway clutching a scattergun in a manner that suggested he'd be happier if it was a skillet of bacon. No chance he was the marshal, Marat thought. Even a drunk numskull like Billy wouldn't have got himself captured by this tubby dolt.

Marat affected to feel a stone in his boot and made a palaver of removing it, all the while making a careful reconnaissance of the jail. The building was made of stout ponderosa logs. Round metal bars and wooden shutters were fitted over all the windows. The front door was made of thick planks of mountain mahogany and looked just about tough enough to bounce away a cannonball. The roof, though, was a different matter. Squatting down to readjust his spurs,

Marat could see that it was flat and made of turf squares laid over spruce poles. Any man with a sharp Bowie knife could cut an exit flap in it in inside of ten minutes. Whistling an old French air his great-grand-daddy had brought with him from Gascony, Marat rose to his feet and sauntered off down the street.

A few hundred yards beyond a newspaper office, whose proprietor stank so strongly of alcohol a man could have got drunk just by sniffing him, Marat encountered a small crowd of people gathered around a couple of salesmen. The men wore fancy Eastern duds. They were peddling perfumes and soaps. Marat stopped for a moment to watch them. He had no interest in what they had to offer, but he liked the rhythm of their patter.

'Ladies, rest assured, our Sheba's Musk of Damask Rose will bewitch every fellow in the room. The merest dab beneath the ears, it is said amongst the Ottoman Turks is enough to make the most pious holy man swoon. Gentlemen, rest assured that you are not neglected. Amongst our wares is one very special preparation. Lasseter and Fields's Rich Almond Moustache and Beard Crème. This lustrous unguent is sworn by not only by the boulevardiers of the metropolis, but also by the frontier forces of justice, right here in this very town. Oh yes, ladies and gentlemen, for didn't we receive only yesterday a glowing encomium to the efficacy of this superior oil from none other than one of our most illustrious US Marshals? 'Sirs,' said this most upright and courageous of gentlemen to Mr Rathbone and myself last evening when we encountered him at Mr Sullivan's fine hotel, 'Let me say that even during the fiercest gun battle with border ruffians never once have I worried about the comeliness of my moustaches, so confident have I been in the properties of your most efficacious and manly preparation.' Yes, indeed, ladies and gentlemen, the words, the very words of Deputy US Marshal Bishop himself.'

When Marat heard Bishop's name he

let out an involuntary exclamation, then covered it with a cough. The Clergyman, *mon Dieu*!

'You indicate surprise, sir,' said Mr Wade, pointing at Marat. 'Yet do not doubt us. For Marshal Bishop is to be located e'en now in Sullivan's Hotel. And such is his commendable commitment to his trade that he asked, nay demanded, that he be given a room overlooking the town jail, that he might reflect upon it and the felons there incarcerated. Were you to go to him this second and demand it, we stand assured that he would respectfully confirm the veracity of our testimony.'

'But if I may place a proviso on my colleague Mr Wade's pronouncement,' Mr Rathbone chimed in, 'if you are to approach the good marshal, pray do so only when he appears to be in the mood to accept visitors. For though we have found this brave gentleman the soul of conviviality, others report that, weighed down by the cares of office, at times less propitious he can be a tad . . . irascible.'

Marat wasn't listening any more, however. He had moved around the edge of the crowd so that he could get a better view of the hotel. One of the windows overlooking the street was open. Poking from it Marat could see what looked very like the barrel of a rifle. So that was it. Longeye's instinct had been right again.

Marat walked back towards the hotel, then ducked down a side alley that took him to an area of cattle and livery pens, outhouses and wooden privies that lay behind the main drag. Steam wafted from the vast tubs of a Chinese laundry that had set up in a tent next to the wagon of an itinerant dentist and barber. Beyond them was a long row of one-room clapboard houses, home to the sporting girls whose silk drawers were flapping on the clothes lines. Clustered beyond were the ridge tents of would-be goldminers taking one last peek at civilization before disappearing into the hills, probably for good.

Marat picked his way over the frozen

ground. Refuse from the various saloons, billiard halls and eating houses had been hurled out from the back entrances. Lop-eared pigs rooted around amongst mounds of mouldering offal and cabbage leaves. Stepping past a fat sow and around a man collapsed face down, either dead drunk or just plain dead, he found his way to the back of Sullivan's Hotel. An exterior staircase led to the first floor from outside the laundry room at the back of the building.

Marat ascended it. The door at the top was locked, but there was a sash window at right angles to it. No lights were on inside. The *Canadien* took the scalping knife from his belt, carefully popped the catch and then gently levered the bottom half of the window upwards until he could get his fingers underneath. When it was open he stuck his head inside. The room smelled powerfully of scent and soap. It was plainly the place where the two salesmen were staying. A door on the far side of the room led out on to the landing beyond.

Across the landing was the door of the room in which Deputy US Marshal Bishop was sitting and waiting to shoot Louis Longeye. Marat smiled to himself. The Clergyman was going to get a surprise later.

A few minutes later Marat stepped out of the alley and on to the boardwalk. He was stomping back towards his horse and mule when, on the opposite side of Lone Pine's Main Street, he saw something that made him stop dead in his tracks.

Walking along past the brandy-stinking newsman was a young woman in a dark blue cape trimmed with pale fur. The woman had blonde hair the colour of pale straw. She was pretty, very pretty with the pale, glowing skin of a plaster angel. Yet it was not the young woman that caught Marat's attention, it was the old man walking beside her. He was tall, slim and erect, his long face framed with a mane of white hair. At the sight of him the sparkle went from Marat's eyes. A dull and brutal menace replaced it.

After waiting until the couple had passed further along the boardwalk, Marat picked his way across the street and followed slowly behind them, his fingers resting on the handle of his scalping knife. The old judge and the woman — his daughter most likely — walked slowly, stopping to look in shop windows and exchange small talk with people as they passed.

Eventually they reached a point in Lone Pine where the storefronts gave way to an area of larger houses. On the porch of one of them a younger man waved to them. As he raised his arm Marat noticed the man's hands. They were twisted like alder twigs. The old judge and the blonde woman went over to chat with Crooked Hands, and Marat filled the time by staring at some saddles in the window of a hardware store, keeping track of the judge via the reflection in the glass.

'I hope we shall see you later this evening, Mr Morgan,' Kitty said as the three of them finished their brief chat and she and her father were turning to go. 'I reckon you will, ma'am,' Morgan said. 'I've much to learn and the judge keeps me to it.'

He watched as Kitty and her father walked away, he noticed out of the corner of his eye that a silver-bearded forty-niner, whose boots didn't seem to fit him too well, was also taking an interest. Still, who could blame him? Kitty surely was a peach.

Marat watched the judge enter a white clapboard two-storey house, then turned and strode briskly back up the street. He no longer noticed the discomfort of the boots or the shirt. He was too filled with rage to notice much at all. Eight years back, in Kansas, Marat and Louis Longeye had been captured by a posse and put on trial for attacking a wagon train of settlers. He could still hear the voice of the presiding judge passing sentence, talking in some soft, syrupy American accent he didn't recognize:

'*Two cold and vicious men, devoid of morality or remorse. I have no hesitation in sentencing you to be hanged and — may I add — the sooner the deed is done the safer and happier this good Earth shall be.'*

But it never got done, neither sooner nor later. Marat stabbed the warder of the jail with a knife he'd fashioned from a dinner spoon. He and Louis bust out, strangled an army sutler, stole his horses and galloped off back to the Black Hills.

They'd got away. But that judge, he'd wanted them dead. And now here the old pig was, walking the streets of Lone Pine like he hadn't a worry in the world. Well, they'd see about that. Sure enough they would.

★   ★   ★

In a grove of burr oaks on a ridge overlooking Lone Pine Louis Longeye stood watching the sun sink behind the craggy outline of the Black Hills. The sky was clear, but the easterly wind carried the smell of approaching snow.

Billy Bearpaw was Louis's brother's child. Joseph Longeye had died in an attack on a Canadian Army munitions convoy. The boy's mother was an Ojibway squaw. When the boy was ten she fell in with some white traders. They gave her whiskey. Later they killed her. What happened in between Louis Longeye did not know and the traders were no longer alive to tell. From the day Billy's mother died the boy became his uncle's responsibility. It had not been easy. The youngster had fallen into the ways of the whitemen — drinking, gambling and chasing women. He had no respect for anything, least of all himself.

Still, Billy was of Longeye's blood and that carried with it a burden, one that could not be thrown off. Louis would do all he could to rescue the youth, whether he was worth rescuing or not. Besides, the information Jack Marat had brought back from the town was better than Louis could have hoped for. Tonight he would settle many old scores.

A flock of crows settled noisily in the spruce trees behind Longeye. The birds' cawing sounded to him like the war cries of long dead warriors — his ancestors and the men they'd fought. The big Metis stooped down and took a handful of earth and pine needles in his hand. His lips moving silently, he tossed the debris high into the evening sky. As it drifted away on the wind he prepared himself — once again — to kill, and to die.

Marat and the rest of the gang were huddled under blankets and skins by the horses. No campfire had been lit. The cold had begun to bite. When the men saw Longeye coming they got to their feet, still clutching the blankets tight around themselves.

'Here is what we do,' Longeye said. 'Henri Youngbuck, take Frank and Emil, Jean and Pierre and go rescue Billy.'

He turned to look at Frank Petty, who was standing on the edge of the group. The mention of his name seemed to send a jolt through the young reprobate, and now, as Louis stared at him, a pallor spread rapidly across his callow face.

'You,' the leader said, 'have got a chance to make good the bad you done. These others stand watch. You make the rescue. Cut through the roof like Jack said and haul Billy up. You got rope on your saddle?'

Petty mumbled that he had.

'Before you go,' Longeye said, 'you need to make yourself look as a warrior should. Put on war paint. Like mine.' He pointed to his face which was daubed white with black streaks. 'Help you hide in the moonlight. Go do it.'

Petty nodded and went off to his horse.

'Me, Jack, the rest, we going to go into that town and create trouble. Draw attention away from the jail. *Comprendez?*'

The gang nodded and murmured assent.

'Get ready,' Longeye said. 'We going to leave first. Henri, you and your boys wait till we gone thirty minutes, then you go.'

Longeye, Marat and the three other members of the gang saddled their horses and mounted up. As they rode off they passed Frank Petty. The youngster's face-paint was an almost perfect replica of the outlaw leader's.

Jack Marat chuckled softly when he saw it. 'You got some cunning in you, *ami*,' he said to Louis. 'No doubt about it.'

When they were a few minutes out of camp Longeye called the party to a halt.

'Jack and me, we got business at the far end of town,' he said. 'Charlie, Manu, Luc, I got a special job for you. Jack going to explain it.'

4

Bishop stubbed out the butt of a cigarillo in what remained of his dinner. The hotel's ill-mannered proprietor had described it as 'Irish stew.' The way the marshal figured it the only thing that made the slop Irish was the fact that some of the meat was green. He picked up the silver flask that sat on the table next to the abandoned meal. His cigar case, binoculars and a neat row of heavy-calibre cartridges were arranged on it also. Bishop took a hearty swig of whiskey. Even though he swirled the liquor round his mouth several times before he swallowed it the sour taste of Sullivan's gravy remained on his tongue.

Night had fallen and a chill wind whipping in from the plains to the east had sent the citizens of Lone Pine scurrying indoors. Main Street was quiet. The only person visible was the sheriff's halfwit son, standing outside his father's office, shivering and fiddling with his pistol. Inside the sheriff was likely sleeping off the effects of a feast. Folk seemed to have been ferrying baskets of chow to him all day long. If he didn't cross the threshold of his office, it was probably only because he was too wide to fit through the door.

Bishop took up his binoculars and scanned the wooded hillside that rose up behind the sheriff's office. By his reckoning Louis Longeye should be just about here. The roof, he knew, was the point of weakness. That was where they'd try to break in. The moon was up. His hotel room was dark. Nobody was around. Everything — except for his stomach — was just the way Bishop had wanted it.

There were some shouts from the room across the hall. No doubt the two travelling salesmen were engaged in an argument over which of them had peddled the most soap. Bishop barely heard it for at that moment he glimpsed some movement amongst the pine trees a hundred yards or so above the jail. Soon he picked out four men, coming gently down the slope, rifles and shotguns cradled in their arms. Leading them, sporting the white-and-black face-paint he always wore in battle, was Louis Longeye.

Bishop slipped out of his chair, picked up the Sharps rifle that was resting against the end of the bed and placed it on the tripod. He moved the barrel slowly until his target was centred in the sight. Louis Longeye came down the slope, moving in a zigzag pattern. Bishop's eye followed him every step. When the outlaw was parallel with the hotel window, about fifty yards away, the deputy US narshal slowly squeezed the trigger.

The report of the heavy buffalo gun reverberated around the room. On the hillside opposite the outlaw staggered briefly, then toppled forward. Gunshots rang wildly out as the rest of the gang fired in Bishop's general direction.

There was no light in the room, and unless they saw the muzzle flash it was unlikely they'd know exactly where the bullet came from. But a lucky shot could kill a man as surely as well-aimed one, and Bishop, pulling the rifle with him, ducked down between the bed and the window ledge.

The decision saved the lawman's life. A split second later the door to his room was kicked open and Charlie Trapper burst in. The outlaw sent two barrels of 0-gauge buckshot raking across the spot Bishop had so recently occupied. The blast sent the gun tripod crashing against the wall and over-turned the table.

From the back of Trapper his cohort Manu Foxtail let fly with a Colt revolver, pumping six .45 slugs into the armchair and sending wood splinters and gouts of horsehair flying. Black powder smoke now hung in a thick pall across the room. Trapper coughed loudly. 'The hell he go?' he asked Foxtail.

Behind the bed Bishop discarded the rifle, quietly drew his Remington revolver and cocked the hammer. As he heard the two felons stepping further into the room, the marshal swung up into a half crouch, got a fix on their position and fired. The first shot struck Trapper in the right shoulder, the second killed him as he spun. Foxtail was struggling to reload his pistol. He'd got two shells in the cylinder before the marshal's third shot hit him in the guts, knocking him back through the doorway and on to the landing.

Bishop got to his feet and strode across the room. From the threshold he put two more bullets into the writhing, squealing form of Foxtail. Behind him he heard gunfire from around the jail, the windows of the hotel shattering and a ragged volley from what he guessed must be the customers at The Dutchman's saloon.

After pausing to snap five shells into the cylinder of the Remington the lawman moved cautiously towards room number four. The door was slightly ajar. From a position to the right Bishop pushed it open with the barrel of his revolver, then ducked back. When no shots came the marshal leaned out across the doorway to get a look inside.

There was nobody in the room. At least, nobody alive. Wade and Rathbone were spread-eagled across their beds. Their throats were slashed and they'd been scalped.

Bishop's eyes narrowed. He glanced around quickly at the corpse on the landing, thinking about the shouts he'd heard just before he spotted the outlaws. The gap between that moment and the two men bursting into his room wasn't sufficient for the pair of them to have killed and then mutilated the salesmen. That meant there were more of them.

Raising the Remington to eye level, Bishop advanced slowly into room four. The window opposite him was wide open and gave access to an exterior staircase. That was how the outlaws had got in. Aside from that the lay-out in four was much the same as that of his room. Twin beds, a cigarette-burned table, armchair, chest of drawers and a double-fronted wardrobe.

With the gun still held in front of him Bishop moved toward the window, stepping quietly, ears pricked to catch any sound. From somewhere across the butchers' pens at the back of the hotel came the sound of a woman laughing. A large dog barked.

When he reached the window Bishop glanced quickly out of it. Looking below he saw horses tethered to the fence of one of the cattle pens. There were three of them.

The marshal turned slowly, scanning the room. He held his breath. From near by he heard the sound of metal on metal. Somebody somewhere was very, very softly turning the handle of a door.

The lawman swung the Remington to his right and fired four shots into the side of the wardrobe. A groan of agony followed. The doors opened and Luc Montreal tumbled out, landing face first on the moth-eaten carpet.

Satisfied that he'd taken care of all the men sent to kill him, Bishop marched briskly back to his room, stepping without a second glance over the corpses of those he'd shot.

Through the shattered window the marshal could see two of Longeye's men on the roof of the jail, cutting at the turf with long-bladed knives. He pulled the blankets off one of the beds and threw them over the glass that covered the floor under the window. He took up the Sharps rifle, he kneeled on the blanket, took a shell from his gunbelt, chambered it and took aim.

When he saw his partner blasted across the roof, the other outlaw did not waste time. He drew a pistol from his belt and snapped off several rounds in the general direction of the hotel. Then he jumped to the ground and disappeared behind the jail.

Bishop reloaded the single-shot rifle

and waited. A few moments later the outlaw darted out from cover and began to run up the hillside. As he drew a bead on the scurrying figure, Bishop noticed movement off to the left of his target. A man in a high-crowned hat had stepped from behind a tree and was aiming a double-barrelled shotgun straight at him. The marshal flung himself to one side as buckshot ripped into the room. Shards of glass from the window frame tore past him and the oil lamp on the chest of drawers exploded, sending crystal and ignited kerosene splattering over the furniture and walls.

When the marshal raised himself to peek out of what remained of the window the two outlaws had gone.

Bishop rose to his feet and surveyed the scene. Shattered glass and debris were everywhere. The flaming lamp oil had burned holes in the carpet and singed the wallpaper, buckshot pellets pitted the furniture. A dead man was slumped against one wall, his blood sprayed across the wallpaper and soaking the floor around him. There was another body on the landing and three more in the room opposite.

Bishop descended the stairs and rang the bell at the reception desk. After a minute Sullivan emerged from the back office scowling. Recent events seemed to have bypassed him completely.

'What d'you want?' he snarled.

The marshal smiled at him. 'Rooms two and four need cleaning,' he said, then turned and walked out into the street.

★　★　★

When Deputy US Marshal Bishop's first rifle shot echoed across Main Street Plug Watson didn't pause to identify where the firing came from. Drawing his shiny new Colt revolver he fired two shots into the sky and leapt into the sheriff's office, slamming the door behind him. 'They're coming, Pa! They're coming to get the outlaw!' he hollered.

The gunfire and yelling woke Sheriff Watson from his post-dinner nap. Leaping to his feet with a grunt he seized his sawed-off shotgun from the desk where it was lying and commenced swinging it about the room. Satisfied no intruders were in the building, he put the gun back down, rubbed the sleep out of his eyes and said,

'Bolt the darn door, son, and quit shouting. Ain't nobody coming for this piece of garbage 'cept the marshal.'

Billy Bearpaw had been lying on his cot in the jail cell, but at the sound of gunfire he'd risen to his feet.

'You wrong,' he said. 'My uncle going to come for me. He's going to take you too. Put you on a spit and roast you over a slow fire like a big juicy pig. We going to be listening to you scream for a long, long time, fat man.'

'Now you just quit that talk, mister,' Plug told him.

Bearpaw walked to the front of the cell. 'Or what, Momma's boy?' he sneered. 'My uncle gonna take you too. Put you in petticoats and sell you to the Lakota as a squaw.' He laughed, 'You make a nice little wife for some brave as ain't too fussy, huh?'

Plug Watson flushed red with rage and embarrassment. 'Why you, you . . .' he spluttered.

'That's enough, son,' Sheriff Watson said, reaching out to pat Plug on the arm. 'This boy here got a nasty mind and a mouth to match. No need for you to go down that same track.'

Plug took a deep breath. 'You're right, Daddy,' he said.

'Yeah, for sure,' Bearpaw said. 'You just listen to Poppa, little missy. Do what he says and maybe he buy you a nice new dress.'

Plug flushed again and reached for his revolver, but a thud on the roof of the building caused him to stop in mid action.

'What was that, Daddy?'

The noise from the roof was followed by another rattle of gunfire.

'I'm in here, boys!' Billy Bearpaw

bellowed, 'Come git me!'

'Nobody's coming to get you, mister,' Sheriff Watson shouted back, but without the same conviction as before. 'Deputy' he commanded Plug, 'make sure all the window shutters are secured.'

As his son busied himself checking the bolts, his father took another shotgun down from the rack behind his desk and loaded it with cartridges from a box in his desk drawer. He pulled the revolver from his holster and flipped out the cylinder to check it was loaded too. As he did so his hand shook and three of the shells fell out on to the floor.

'Not so brave now, huh, fat man?' Billy jeered.

The sheriff ignored the taunt and bent down to retrieve the ammunition. As he gathered the shells soil, dirt and plaster fell from the ceiling on to the surface of his desk.

'By Jiminy, Daddy. Look!' Plug yelped, pointing upwards. The shining steel tip of a 12-inch blade Bowie knife protruded from the ceiling. It withdrew, and then emerged again a few inches further on, sending another shower of debris on to Watson's desk. 'They're cutting through the roof!' the boy squealed.

Sheriff Watson responded by firing the sawed-off at the spot where the knife had just reappeared. The shot brought down more of the roof, but the blade was back again a split second later. The turf sods had absorbed the buckshot. The sheriff now emptied his revolver into the ceiling too, but the knife kept working.

'They're still there. They're still there. What are we going to do, Daddy?' Plug jabbered.

'Know what I'm gonna do,' Billy Bearpaw shouted. 'Gonna slit your throat just to stop your bawling.'

'You're making me mad, mister,' Plug shouted back. His eyes were wild and there were tears in them. He drew his pistol and advanced towards the cell.

'Why, I've a good mind . . . '

His father might have intervened but at that point he was too absorbed trying to reload his weaponry with trembling hands to see what was going on.

' . . . A good mind . . . to shoot you dead right now,' Plug Watson said.

'Come on then, little missy,' Bearpaw leered at him, his face pressed between the bars of the cell.

Outside, gunfire echoed across Main Street. Bullets slapped into the solid wooden sides of the sheriff's office and smashed the panes on the other side of the shutters.

Finally finished reloading, the sheriff began once again firing into the ceiling. The knife kept coming without hesitation.

When Plug Watson was standing right in front of him, the prisoner spat into his face. A great gob of spittle struck the deputy on his right cheek. Face contorted in revulsion, he reached up to wipe it away.

The next thing Plug knew Bearpaw

had reached out from between the bars, grabbed the barrel of the pistol and was trying to twist it from his grasp.

'Let go, you . . . ' Plug squeaked, and he reached out to put two hands on the pistol. Bearpaw kept pulling and twisting. He was much stronger than his opponent. As he tugged the deputy edged close enough to the cell for the outlaw to shoot out his free hand and grab a hold of his belt. Watson yelled in panic. He closed his eyes and fought back with all his strength but, inch by inch, Bearpaw pulled him nearer.

Suddenly there was a loud explosion. The tugging on Watson's belt and pistol stopped. When he opened his eyes, the revolver in his hand was smoking. Billy Bearpaw was staring at him through fearful eyes. The prisoner's hands were pressed to his chest, red oozing from between the fingers.

Plug Watson looked down at the gun. His finger was pressed on the trigger. He looked up again at Bearpaw. The prisoner had sunk to his knees, his forehead resting on the bars of the cell.

Sheriff Watson discharged six more shots into the ceiling. The knife disappeared and this time it did not return. The sheriff waited. Still the knife did not come.

'We did it, son,' the sheriff called out, his voice exultant with triumph and relief. 'They've gone. We've whipped them!'

But his son didn't answer. He was looking down at the body of Billy Bearpaw and weeping.

★　★　★

Morgan was sitting by the stove in the little front sitting room of Widow Jennings's boarding house. He'd eaten a good dinner of braised beef, finished off with apple pie. The combination of a full stomach, the warmth from the stove and the thudding dullness of *Blackwood* was making his eyes feel real heavy. He was struggling to his feet with a view to stepping out on to the porch and letting the freezing night air sharpen his mind when he heard the shot.

Gunfire was not unusual in Lone Pine, especially on Friday and Saturday nights. The high-spirited and the crazy drunk tended to discharge six-guns, though, and the shot that had just echoed down Main Street came from a heavy-calibre rifle.

Outside on the front porch Morgan felt the freezing cold slap into his lungs. The rifle shot had drawn a response from what sounded like a shotgun and now pistol fire rattled out from the general direction of The Dutchman's saloon. He had expected the volume to lessen once the miscreants responsible got the devilment out of their systems. When it continued unabated, Morgan went upstairs to arm himself.

The law student's bedroom was spotlessly clean and methodically arranged. Legal tomes in alphabetical order filled a high shelf above the dressing table, a pair of highly polished boots stood at the end of an immaculately made bed.

A sharply pressed Sunday best suit hung on the wall above it. The neatness was a legacy of his army days. Morgan clung fiercely to the rules and regulations of that time. He had reason to. Back after the snowstorm had crippled him, he'd lost himself in self-pity, drinking and degradation. Judge Persimmon had rescued him. The former marshal had been arraigned before him on charges of public drunkenness and affray. Recognizing Morgan as a man who had served the court well in the past, Judge Persimmon ordered the ex-marshal released on condition he called on him every evening. Since that time Morgan had stuck to a straight and narrow path. He knew that if he ever stepped off it, even a little way, he'd likely fall into the darkness once more. Maybe this time for good.

Morgan kept his weaponry in a drawer of the dressing-table. Morgan kept the drawer locked because the guns inside were loaded. With his crooked fingers the former marshal struggled to reload at speed. On the one occasion he'd dared to time himself it had taken a little under five minutes to fill the six-shot cylinder on a revolver. Long enough for any foe to kill him ten times over.

He unlocked the drawer with a key he'd fitted into a wide wooden handle for ease of grip and took inventory of his arsenal. Aside from the pepperbox pistol with which he'd faced down Bishop, the drawer contained a chrome-plated Smith & Wesson New Model Number 3 six-shooter with a top-break system that allowed a man to empty spent shells one-handed, and a sawed off 10-gauge shotgun with the stock refashioned as a pistol grip. Both weapons had the trigger guards removed so that Morgan could fire them and both nestled in the holsters of a custom-made gunbelt. Morgan buckled the belt with some effort, took a thick green plaid cattleman's jacket from the hook behind the bedroom door and tugged it on. He had reached the foot of the stairs and was pulling on his Stetson, when he heard the scream. Racing to Widow Jennings's front door he flung it open and, looking across the street, saw the figure of a man disappearing through one of the downstairs windows of the Persimmon house.

Heart racing, Morgan rushed across to the gate of the judge's home and moved stealthily up the path to the main entrance. Lights were on inside. Morgan thought he could hear muffled shouts coming from the rear of the building.

He paused for a moment, thinking, then drew the sawed-off scattergun, kicked open the front door with the flat of his right boot and lunged inside, the gun held at hip level. As he entered the lobby he saw a silver-bearded fellow in woodsman's buckskins running up the main staircase. When the intruder reached the landing, Morgan raised his weapon and fired both barrels. The man seemed to sense what was coming. He dived to the floor a fraction of a second before the gun discharged. With a

deafening roar buckshot r
deep red Regency strip
which Kitty was so p
leapt to his feet the m
off had fired and disap
corridor that led to the s
ters. Morgan slotted the sawed-
in the holster and drew his revolver.
was preparing to ascend the stairs when
he heard Judge Persimmon yelling from
the kitchen.

'Oh yes,' the judge shouted, 'I'd find
it impossible to forget you, even if I
wanted to. And God knows there's
reason enough for that, you blood-
thirsty cur.'

Holding the pistol against his side
Morgan advanced down the corridor,
recalling that the last time he'd been in
this house Kitty was walking down it
carrying a vase of dried lavender.

He passed the closed door to the
dining room. The entrance to the sitting
room was open and a chill breeze blew
in from the window through which the
villains had entered. From the kitchen

d a low, deep voice snarling in
se. Morgan stepped into the
way, raising the Smith & Wesson.
dge Persimmon was tied to a chair.
here were slash marks on both of his
cheeks. The man who had made them
was standing to the judge's left, a long
knick-bladed steel knife in his fist. He
was a huge beast of fellow with massive
shoulders and thick arms straining against
the buckskin of his fringed jerkin. Long
black hair framed a solid, rectangular
face painted white, with dark streaks
running across it like the marks on the
trunk of a silver birch.

'Many men you hang, white-hair,' the
big man growled in broken English.
'Now you get taste of how it feels.'

'No, I don't think so,' Morgan said.
At the sound of his voice the intruder
twisted to face the speaker.

'Shoot him, Isaac,' the judge cried
when he saw his student. 'Kill him while
you have the chance.' But before Morgan
could pull the trigger the outlaw leapt
away to his right, disappearing from his

view behind a high dresser, stacked with blue-and-white crockery. Despite his size the man moved with the nimble agility of an antelope.

Morgan stepped further into the room, twisting to see where the big man had gone. As he did so he felt something brush against his arm. There was a heavy thud. Glancing down Morgan saw a slash across the left sleeve of his coat. A long knife was embedded three inches into the clapboard of the kitchen wall.

Enraged, the former lawman fired three shots in the direction from which the knife had come. Even as he pulled the trigger he knew his bullets wouldn't find their target. Beyond the tall dresser was a door into the still room and pantry. The outlaw was holed up in there.

'You bearing up, Judge?' Morgan asked quietly, eyes fixed on the pantry door.

The judge nodded. 'That's Louis Longeye,' he whispered. 'Keep your wits about you, Isaac, or he'll kill you for sure.'

'He's cornered right now,' Morgan said. 'I'll cut you free.'

'Forget about me,' the judge said. 'The other one, Marat . . . he's gone after Kitty. She's upstairs.'

'I can't leave you like this,' Morgan said, but the judge brushed aside his protest.

'I'm an old man, Isaac. Save Kitty. Please!' he beseeched.

With reluctance Morgan turned away from Persimmon, moved quickly down the corridor and up the staircase, pistol poised.

The layout of the upstairs of the house mirrored that of the lower floor. Rooms led off a central passageway, four in total, and at the rear were a washroom and servants' quarters.

On reaching the top of the stairs Morgan paused and listened. When he heard nothing, he leapt out into the door-way, firing two shots high into the ceiling in the hope of distracting anyone who lay in ambush, without risk to Kitty. No muzzle flash answered. The passageway was empty and dark. Either the lamps had not been lit, or someone had extinguished them.

Morgan stepped into the corridor and stood for a moment, his eyes adjusting to the gloom. Objects slowly began to emerge from the shadows — a small table with a jug and washbasin on it, a ladder-back chair. Morgan noticed that the door of the rear bedroom on the right was open. Moonlight came softly through it, illuminating a crumpled garment that lay on the polished oak floor.

Morgan stepped lightly down the corridor, ears straining for any sound. Somewhere along here was Kitty. Somewhere too was the man named Marat.

The doors of the first two bedrooms were closed. Morgan moved past them towards the crumpled garment. As he got nearer to it he recognized the dark blue hooded cape Kitty had been wearing that morning when she and the judge had paused to talk with him on the porch of Widow Jennings's house. As he recalled that scene he remembered the awkward-looking forty-niner with the silver hair who looked uncomfortable in his boots and shirt — like he'd have been happier in buckskins.

Morgan pressed his torso against the wall opposite the open door and slid along it. From somewhere he heard a muffled cry. Was it Kitty or the judge down below? In the echoing house it was impossible to tell. When he was level with the discarded cloak he raised his revolver and advanced boldly into the bedroom. Inside he saw overturned furniture. The shards of a smashed vase and dried lavender flowers were strewn across the floor beneath the window. Morgan glanced from left to right. The room was empty.

He heard a noise behind him, the click of a door handle and a stifled squeak.

'You lost something, *ami?*' a gruff, heavily accented voice enquired from behind him. 'Maybe I found it for you. Turn around. Slowly now.'

Morgan did as he was told. In the corridor he saw Marat. The outlaw had his right arm around Kitty Persimmon, the point of a knife pressed to her pale throat. His left arm held one of her hands behind her back. The young woman's blue eyes were wide with terror and her cheek was reddened from a slap.

Marat grinned triumphantly, a gold incisor glinting in the moonlight.

'Better drop the gun, *monsieur*.'

Morgan did not drop the gun. Instead he raised it, slowly and surely, until he was looking along the gleaming barrel of the Smith & Wesson and straight into outlaw's right eye.

'You're making a big mistake, Yankee.' Marat snarled defiantly, but the flashing tooth had disappeared.

'I don't think so,' Morgan said, his voice not much more than a whisper. 'In a race between a bullet and a man's hand, the bullet wins every time.' He took a step towards Marat. 'But maybe you know different?'

The silver-haired outlaw was eight feet away. Kitty Persimmon was several inches shorter than her captor, giving Morgan a clear view of most of his head. He had no doubt he could hit Marat without harming the girl. He had practised shooting for hours with the customized weapons. Accuracy was not his problem, speed was.

'You think you can shoot straight with those bent-up fingers?' Marat asked, shuffling backwards into the corridor.

'I know it,' Morgan hissed. He began squeezing the unguarded trigger of his revolver.

A guttural shout came from the bottom of the stairs. It was Longeye.

'I hear one shot and the judge dies,' he bellowed. 'He is right here, Crooked Hands. Tell him, judge.'

There was a groan and then Judge Persimmon called out weakly, 'It's true. But save Ki . . . '

Whatever he had been planning to

add was cut short by a thudding blow.

Kitty Persimmon cried out, 'Don't hurt Father!' Then she turned her flushed face to Morgan. 'Please, Isaac,' she pleaded, 'do as they say. Don't let them harm him.' Reluctantly Morgan lowered the gun.

'You going to drop it now, like I asked before?' Marat said. The grin was back. Morgan narrowed his eyes.

'I don't believe I will,' he replied.

'But you heard what Louis said,' Marat responded, stepping back further into the corridor, dragging Kitty with him.

'Yes,' Morgan said. 'But the way I reckon it is this: if I drop the gun you and your friend downstairs will kill all three of us and walk away free and easy. Whereas, if I hold on to the gun . . . well, then I can even things up a little, one way or another.'

'Please, Isaac . . . ' Kitty sobbed.

'The little lady here, she don't like your arithmetic, *mon frère*,' Marat said, manoeuvring Kitty away from Morgan and towards the stairs. 'You let me and Louis walk away, we won't harm anyone. I give you my word.'

Morgan laughed mirthlessly. 'Your word?' he repeated and stepped forward to reclose the gap between himself and the outlaw.

'You hear me,' Marat said. He was halfway down the corridor now, about ten feet from the doorway to the stairs. 'My oath.'

Morgan watched him. The outlaw and his captive were edging closer to the doorway. If he shot Marat now he could save Kitty, but downstairs Longeye would slaughter the judge and flee. However, if he let Marat out on to the stairs and then followed him, he'd risk being shot by Longeye. And if Morgan was dead, then he had no doubt that Kitty and her father would follow him. He recalled what the judge had said about men like Ambrose Bishop — how they calculated probabilities. He knew that, had he been cut from the same cloth as the deputy US marshal, he'd weigh up the current odds and pick the only deal that guaranteed him some kind of pay out. He'd shoot Marat. But, as the judge had gently pointed out last night, Morgan just wasn't that kind of man.

As Marat reached the threshold of the doorway on to the stairs Morgan raised his weapon again.

'Longeye,' he shouted, 'this is former US Marshal Isaac Morgan speaking. I'm in position to blow your friend's brains all over the wall. You want me to do that, you just say the word. Before you do, I have another choice for you. You let the judge go, step right away from him. Your friend here can take the young lady as far as the front door. Then he leaves her there and the two of you can walk away alive and unharmed. How does that sound?'

'Why should I trust you, Crooked Hands?' Longeye shouted back. 'Every promise Yankees made you broke.'

'Well,' Morgan said, 'see, the way it is, you can trust me and maybe I'll let you and your friend escape. Or you can not trust me and I'll shoot him for certain and, if you're not out of that front door mighty fast, I'll kill you too. See what I'm saying? Trust me and maybe live. Or don't trust me and surely die. That's your choice.'

Marat looked at Morgan, then glanced down at Louis. Luckily neither of the outlaws seemed to have spotted the flaw in Morgan's plan: he only had one bullet left in his six-gun.

'All right, Crooked Hands. I do as you say,' Longeye called from the entrance hall. 'I step away to the door now.'

'He doing that, Judge?' Morgan shouted.

'He is, Isaac. He is indeed,' the judge hollered in response. 'He's at the door now. He's opened it and stepped outside.'

'No funny business,' Morgan said to Marat as the silver-haired woodsman began to back slowly down the stairs with Kitty.

Morgan moved on to the landing and looked down. The judge, dishevelled and pale-faced from his ordeal, was seated on the floor with his hands tied behind his back. The front door of the house was open and Longeye was nowhere to be seen.

'Keep moving along slowly,' Morgan said to Marat, his revolver still trained on the outlaw's head.

He followed Marat and Kitty down the stairs and across the entrance hall, stopping as he came level with the judge. 'Now, Marat,' he said, 'you take the lady into the doorway with you, then you just duck away and leave her there and I won't come after you.'

'All right, *ami*.' Marat replied. As he reached the door he did just as Morgan had said.

After Marat had released his grip on her Kitty Persimmon stood in the front doorway, looking at Morgan. She was framed in the moonlight, her golden hair glowing and, as their eyes met, Morgan felt sure everything was going to work out fine, not just tonight, but for ever. Then a dark hand shot out of the darkness, grabbed the young woman's arm and pulled her swiftly into the night.

By the time Morgan had rushed across the room and out of the doorway, Kitty and her captors had disappeared into the shadows.

5

When Marat grabbed the yellow-haired woman from the doorway she'd been feisty. She'd lashed out with her sharp nails, and even tried to bite his forearm. He'd told her that wasn't ladylike. She kept on kicking, though. Then Louis hit her on the base of the skull with the handle of his knife. That shut her up real quick. Now she was bound with leather thongs and gagged with a strip of birch bark and slung across the front of the saddle of Marat's strawberry roan pony. She wasn't dressed for the outdoors so he'd thrown a tan wool blanket over her. From a distance it looked like he was carrying a dead deer back to camp.

From the scrub brush where they'd tethered the horses, Marat and Louis Longeye rode north, gradually ascending into the hills. When they reached the top of a low, pine-covered ridge they turned west, picking their way upward through trees and clusters of granite boulders until they reached a narrow trail. Below it a cliff, thirty feet in height, dropped away into the forest. Aside from the occasional hoot of a snowy owl or the yelp of a coyote the land was silent.

The two men did nothing to disturb the peace. That was Longeye's choice. Marat had wanted to leave the girl somewhere, ride back into Lone Pine and finish what they'd started. That crook-fingered Yankee had pricked his pride, training a gun on him like that. He wanted to teach him a lesson. Longeye had other ideas. What they were the gang-leader wasn't yet saying. Marat knew him well enough not to bother asking. Louis would tell it when he was ready.

The outlaws rode on until they neared a clearing flanked to the north by huge grey boulders where bald eagles nested. Longeye motioned for them to halt. When they had he put his hands to his mouth and emitted a perfect imitation of the call of the whippoorwill. He did it twice more and waited. When the answering calls came back they rode on.

In the clearing three riders were waiting for them, Henri Youngbuck, Pierre Gazon and Jean Moosejaw. Three riderless ponies, one behind each mounted man, indicated their mission had not been a success.

'Billy?' Longeye asked.

'We were ambushed,' Youngbuck replied. 'A man with a buffalo gun. He shot from a window. Frank and Emil are dead.'

'Sorry to hear that,' Marat said. 'Emil was a good man.'

'A man shooting from a window?' Longeye asked. 'He stopped the five of you busting out Billy? *One man?*'

Youngbuck flushed. 'Hell, he was a deadeye, Louis. Got that big old Sharps. Hollow point bullets. Blew a hole in Frank looked like a bear cave. No way we could get Billy out, was there?' He looked around for support from his two companions. They both had their gaze fixed firmly on the ground.

'The shooting finished one time,' Youngbuck continued, desperate to convince with his alibi. 'We thought maybe he was hit. Emil and Jean were cutting through the roof like you said. Then the shooting with the buffalo rifle started again. That was when Emil stopped one.'

'The shooting finish, then start again?' Longeye asked.

'Like I say,' Youngbuck replied. 'If it had stopped a while longer we'd have sprung Billy for sure. But that gunman he was a sure shot, Louis. On my mother's grave he was. Nothing we could do. Nothing.'

Longeye made no comment. 'We go back to camp,' he said, and dug his heels into the flanks of his mare.

'What about Charlie, Manu and Luc?' Youngbuck asked. 'We waiting for them?'

'They not coming back, *ami*,' Marat replied, and he followed Longeye up along the trail.

The ground was rocky and the ponies picked their way jumpily along it. The woman slung across Marat's saddle stirred slightly, like she was dreaming. She muttered something, moved again, and then stopped. Marat patted the blanket. He could feel her warmth even through the thick wool. She was a pretty girl. He remembered her blue eyes when he had seen her in the street, and the rose scent of her yellow hair when he had held the knife to her throat at the judge's house. If Louis didn't want the woman, maybe he could keep her. He already had Two Birds, but there was room in his wigwam for more than one squaw.

They had ridden for five minutes, climbing higher into the hills, when Longeye raised his hand for the band to stop. They halted and listened. The horses snorted clouds of steamy breath into the chilled night air. Somewhere far off a wolf howled. Then Marat heard it. From a half-mile or so to the south came the sound of a man drunkenly singing. The man's voice was a loud tenor. He was singing about taking a woman named Kathleen home again. Well, Marat thought that was never going to happen now.

★ ★ ★

Col McCool had reason to feel his luck had changed. A lifetime living in poverty in Ireland had driven him to take a storm-tossed trip across the Atlantic. New York had been seething with disease. Jobs had been few and far between. The wagon train West had been a bumping nightmare that had lasted several weeks and eaten up all his savings. Then, on the Irishman's second day of prospecting, he was panning for gold in a river locals called Brokehope Creek and within twenty minutes he'd turned up a nugget the size of a bantam's egg.

The bespectacled fellow in Lone Pine's assay office had inspected the nugget with a magnifying glass, tested it for brittleness, weighed it, measured it and pronounced it good. He handed McCool more money than the Irishman had ever seen in his life. Twelve hours later he'd spent half of it on drink and women, and wasted a good chunk of the rest.

Col McCool had been in The Dutchman's saloon most of that day. He was losing coins at Faro and wondering if the piano-man was ever going to play 'Danny Boy', when the gunfire brought his celebrations to a halt. From what the Irishman could make out the shooting came from over on the other side of the street — far enough away to be none of his business.

The Irishman was considering ordering another bottle of whiskey. Maybe seeing if the big brunette in the red frock might be interested in helping him drink it, when some idiot yelled, 'It's a jailbreak!'

Next thing Col knew men all around him were brandishing their firing irons. A bullet from somewhere shattered the front window of the saloon. After that pistol shots rattled out on all sides. Most went into the walls and ceiling. The girls yelped and ran for cover. The piano player abandoned *The Battle Hymn of the Republic* and ducked down beneath the keyboard. When a slug ricocheted into the shelving behind the bar, destroying several bottles of brandy, the big bartender with the walrus 'tache pulled a sawed-off shotgun from beneath the counter. Waving it above his head he bellowed that the next man who damaged The Dutchman's property was going to end up leaking beer from a hundred holes. The shooting was a good deal more discriminate after that. Still, for McCool it had put a dampener on the evening. He decided to vacate the scene and clear his head with a moonlit stroll in the hills. It was the sort of thing he'd have done after a night in the pub in his native Galway. But Col

McCool was not in Ireland any more.

The prospector was relieving himself against the trunk of a handsome Black Hills spruce tree and singing about the Rose of Tralee when he heard the rifle hammer cocked behind him.

'You have powerful lungs, *ami*,' a rough voice said. 'Don't make me have to burst them, heh? Finish what you doing, then put your hands in the air and turn around slow.'

★ ★ ★

Isaac Morgan had run out on to the porch the moment Kitty Persimmon had been snatched. Oak trees surrounded the judge's house. The leafless winter branches cast stark shadows in the moonlight, which confused Morgan's vision. He saw footmarks on the frost and followed them carefully. Somewhere out in the night Longeye and Marat could be waiting in ambush. The Smith & Wesson revolver was in his hand, but with only one shell in the cylinder it was more for show than fighting.

As Morgan rounded a cluster of bushes he caught sight of the outlaws up ahead. Longeye was on his horse and already trotting away to the north. Marat was busily lashing something to the front of his saddle. Morgan raised the gun to shoot. He was squeezing the trigger when it dawned on him that the long, limp object across the outlaw's mount was Kitty. Indoors at five yards range he'd have backed himself to miss the woman and hit her captor every time. Here, in the moonlight, at forty paces, he couldn't be so confident. As Marat pulled himself into the saddle and turned the horse northward, Morgan reluctantly lowered his gun and watched with impotent rage as the villain and his captive disappeared into the darkness.

Back in the Persimmon home, Morgan freed the judge from his bindings. The cuts on his cheeks were superficial. They'd likely heal without scarring. As the judge massaged the circulation back into his hands Morgan went to the study. He came back carrying two restorative glasses of bourbon. From Main Street the sound of gunfire could still be heard.

'There's a lot of lead being slung up there,' Morgan said. The judge took a long drink of the whiskey and gasped slightly as the warming liquid hit his throat.

'I think I know the reason for that,' he said.

Morgan looked at him enquiringly.

'Longeye mentioned it when he was trussing me up,' the judge said. 'You wanted to hang me,' he said, 'and I guess now you're fixing to hang my nephew, too, heh?' I figure,' the judge continued, 'That must be the boy they've got in the jail. The one Marshal Bishop brought in. Longeye's gang are trying to spring him.'

Morgan scratched his chin. 'Why'd the marshal leave the boy here for the night? It would have been safer to take him back to Yankton this morning. It seems kind of negligent for a man of

Bishop's reputation.'

The judge smiled. 'In matters such as this I doubt Bishop ever acts thoughtlessly, Isaac,' he said. 'I'd wager the situation is exactly as he would have chosen it, with one or two exceptions.'

'What do you mean?' Morgan asked.

The judge set his empty whiskey glass down on the oak floor. 'Bishop knew Longeye was bound by blood to come and attempt a rescue of his nephew. I'd guess he planned to bushwhack him. If you want to catch a mountain lion you have to find a goat as bait. Something went wrong, though. Instead of going to the jail, Longeye came here. Though how he knew where to find me — '

'Marat!' Morgan cut him off. 'He was in town yesterday, though I didn't know who he was then. I saw him standing over by Hubbock's saddlery, watching you and Kitty . . . ' As he said the young woman's name Morgan's face flushed with anger and humiliation. 'I'm sorry, judge. I let you down.'

The judge reached over and grasped Morgan firmly by the arm. 'You didn't let anyone down, Isaac,' he said. 'If you hadn't come by when you did Kitty and I would both be dead — of that I'm certain. As it is we are both alive and will be yet, I'm sure.' The judge squeezed Morgan's forearm. 'Will you get Kitty back for me, Isaac?' he demanded.

Morgan looked into the judge's eyes. They were the same bright blue as those of his daughter.

'You know I will, Judge,' he said. 'You know I will.'

★   ★   ★

Deputy US Marshal Ambrose Bishop stepped out on to the sidewalk from Sullivan's Hotel, turned left and walked to The Dutchman's saloon. From inside came hollers, howls and gunfire. As he walked Bishop transferred the Buffalo rifle to his left hand and drew his Remington.

Holding the pistol up by the side of

his head Bishop kicked open the doors of the saloon. As he stepped into the fog of powder smoke he was already bellowing.

'I am Deputy US Marshal Ambrose Bishop,' he shouted. 'Any man who discharges a firearm in my presence will be regarded as hostile.' Bishop looked fiercely around the smoke-filled saloon at the dirty, drink-hazy faces of its patrons and raised his pistol so that all of them got a good look at it.

It took a particular type of man to stare down a barroom filled with drunk and fired up frontiersmen. Bishop was such a man. Within seconds of his announcement the violent hubbub in the saloon had dropped to a whisper and pistols were being holstered.

'Your cooperation is appreciated, gentlemen,' Bishop said, turned on his heels and walked out.

The deputy US marshal strode across the street towards the jail, and then past it through the narrow cut that separate the building from the neighbouring dry-goods store. With long energetic strides he began to climb the hill. He paused briefly to look at the body of Emil Maquereau and scowled slightly. The heavy-calibre Sharps bullet had hit the outlaw in the left side of the chest. Bishop had been aiming for his heart. He made a note to adjust his rifle sight and stalked further up the rise until he came to the first outlaw he'd shot.

The body was sprawled by a pine stump. Both arms were flung back, the left leg bent at an unnatural angle. Even from ten yards away Bishop knew it was not the man he wanted. The dead outlaw had the black-and-white face paint that Louis Longeye wore in battle, but he was too short and slight to be the gang leader. When Bishop reached the body he crouched down and examined one of the hands. Louis Longeye was in his middle forties. This was a young man's palm. Looking closely at the face and clothes Bishop saw that the corpse belonged to Billy Bearpaw's one-time companion, Frank.

The deputy US marshal rose to his feet. When most men realize that their carefully laid schemes have been thwarted they curse, or spit. Bishop did neither of these things. Setting his jaw firmly he simply walked back down the hillside while sifting through the known facts in an attempt to identify what had gone wrong.

By the time he had reached the boardwalk again he had come to some preliminary conclusions. The surprise attack on his hotel room meant Longeye knew he was here. That was why Longeye had not taken part in the attack on the jail. But the outlaw chief had not been with those who broke into his bedroom. Nor had his lieutenant Marat been present in either place. Bishop concluded that he did not yet have the complete picture.

As he crossed the street he heard somebody shouting his name, looked to his left and saw that Isaac Morgan was marching up the street towards him. From the look on the man's face

Bishop judged that he was planning to exchange more than just small talk.

★ ★ ★

As Morgan gave his solemn vow to Judge Persimmon it came into his mind that the whole situation was the responsibility of Deputy US Marshal Ambrose Bishop. The lawman had used Lone Pine to snare his quarry. In doing so he'd jeopardized the lives of everyone who lived in the town. And that included Kitty.

As rapidly as his twisted fingers and his rage would allow, Morgan reloaded his pistol and the sawed-off shotgun. Judge Persimmon saw his student's anger.

'Is there something on your mind, Isaac?' he asked.

'Bishop,' Morgan responded curtly, 'This darn mess is his responsibility.'

'Now, Isaac,' the judge said, 'leaving aside the accuracy or otherwise of that statement, do you think Kitty will be best served by you picking a fight with a man such as he?'

Morgan knew that the judge was right, yet he also knew that Bishop was wrong. 'He's put innocent townsfolk at risk just to try and get his job done,' Morgan said. 'Someone needs to put him straight about a few things.'

'This man, Isaac,' the judge protested, 'is not the kind who'll take to being reprimanded, however well merited the case . . . '

Morgan did not wait for the old man to finish. Rising from his chair and holstering the reloaded side arms he said, 'Whether he likes it or whether he doesn't is not my concern. Don't worry, Judge, nothing, not Bishop, Longeye or the entire Sioux Nation, will stop me getting Kitty back.'

Lone Pine's Main Street was quiet again, though the acrid smell of cordite still hung in the frosty air and Gus the barkeep could be seen sweeping up broken glass in front of The Dutchman's saloon. Morgan was passing the offices of the *Clarion* when Bishop stepped out from the alleyway between the sheriff's office and Overbay's store. At the sight of the tall moustachioed lawman the rage rose in him again. Calling the deputy US marshal's name, he strode angrily towards him.

Bishop watched Morgan steadily as he approached. 'You have something on your mind, Mr Morgan?' he enquired politely.

Morgan stopped three feet from the deputy US marshal. 'Too right I do,' he hissed. 'What in damnation makes you think you can ride into town and endanger the lives of everyone here?'

'I don't believe that is what I have done,' Bishop replied evenly.

Morgan laughed sourly. 'Oh, you don't, don't you? You put that boy you caught in the jail here just to lure Louis Long-eye into town. What did you think would happen when he came? You put inno-cent folk at risk.'

'I can see why you might think that, Mr Morgan,' Bishop responded. 'But it's not how I view things. I've been hunting Longeye for five years.' The marshal's eyes narrowed, but he spoke as quietly and evenly as ever. 'During that time his gang has killed more than one hundred people. That's the victims I know of. Should he live another five years how many more will he kill? I calculate it this way: I risked the lives of two local lawmen in order to save those of scores of settlers.'

'But it didn't work, did it?' Morgan growled, 'Longeye's still out there and he's holding a white woman captive. He and Marat took the judge's daughter.'

Bishop tilted his head slightly. 'I wasn't aware of that,' he commented coolly. 'But I know six of the outlaw gang are dead. I know that because I killed them. I miscalculated, Mr Morgan, but I'm still ahead in this game.'

Morgan reddened. 'This game? Darn it, Bishop, these are people you're talking about, not poker chips.' He stepped forward till he was only a foot away from the marshal. 'I ought to have shot you when I had the chance,' he hissed.

Bishop smiled pleasantly. 'And when was that?' he replied, and in the time it took for his smile to widen enough to show a row of sharp, uneven teeth he'd whipped out the Remington revolver, cocked the hammer and jammed the business end of it into Morgan's belly button.

'When you popped out that pepper-box pistol, Mr Morgan,' he said, 'I had good reason not to respond. Circumstances have changed. You want to throw down on me again, be my guest.'

Morgan felt the pressure of the steel barrel against his stomach increase. Anger rose inside him. He fought it down.

'I gave Judge Persimmon my word I'd get his daughter back,' he said, the tone of his voice unaltered by the situation. 'I intend to honour that pledge. And I'm not going to do it with a bullet in my guts.'

'That is a sound assumption,' Bishop said gently, and he reholstered the pistol with the same nonchalant speed with which he'd drawn it. 'Are you intending to attempt this rescue all on your own?'

Morgan looked at him. 'If you're volunteering as my assistant, the answer is no,' he replied curtly. 'You're not interested in rescuing Miss Persimmon. You only care about killing Longeye.'

Bishop smiled again. 'I don't see that those two aims are incompatible,' he said.

Morgan was about to respond when the sound of a horse galloping in from the west end of Main Street distracted him. Both he and Bishop turned to look. The sight that greeted them would have chilled the spines of men less experienced in the vicious ways of the frontier. The horse was a skewbald pony, its flanks decorated with blood-red handprints. Mounted on it was a gory half-living creature that had once been Col McCool.

As the wild-eyed pony approached Bishop stepped calmly out in front of it, drew his revolver and fired once into the air. The pony juddered to a halt. As it flailed its head from side to side looking for a direction in which to flee, the marshal took a few slow paces forward, holstering his pistol as he did so, and seized the rope halter with both hands. The pony attempted to rear, but Bishop's powerful arms held it down.

'There now,' he said in a low soothing voice, as the pony continued to struggle. 'There now, girl.'

A couple of minutes later the pony was sufficiently calm for Bishop to lead her to the hitching rail outside the jail and tether her.

During the entire scene the rider had stared straight ahead, his eyes blank. Evidence of the nightmare torment inflicted on him was all too plainly to be seen across his naked torso.

'Is he alive?' Morgan asked, as Bishop moved to pull the unfortunate Irishman from the back of the pony.

'Yes, though not as you or I would understand the term,' Bishop replied grimly. Gently he lifted the cut and bruised form of Col McCool down and laid him on the sidewalk.

'I'll get Doc Turner,' Morgan said. As he turned to go, the lips of the tortured man began to move.

'Louis Longeye,' he murmured, 'sent a message to . . . the Clergyman . . . '

With a struggle he raised his mangled right hand. In it was a roll of deerskin. Bishop gently took the message from the Irishman's bloody grip.

Col McCool opened his mouth again, but if there was any more of the message he did not deliver it. His ordeal was over.

Bishop, who had been kneeling down beside the wounded man, removed his Mosby hat and clasped it over his chest as he rose slowly to his feet. For a brief moment his face softened.

The flinty look returned as the deputy US marshal unrolled and read the message out loud. It was written with Col McCool's blood.

'Clergyman and Crooked Hands,' he

read, 'bring Bearpaw to the Wolfhead Boulder where the Snake Horn River forks. Two moons from now. Longeye swap white woman for him. The two of you only. Any tricks she die.'

The lawman rolled the message up again. 'Looks like you're going to be riding into the Black Hills with me after all, Mr Morgan,' Bishop said.

If Morgan had a comment to make he didn't get a chance to utter it. At that moment there came from the sheriff's office the sound of heavy locks being unbolted. The door opened a crack and the barrel of a shotgun appeared through it.

'You friend or foe?' called Sheriff Watson, nervously.

'It's Isaac Morgan,' Morgan called back. 'And Marshal Bishop. The outlaws have gone.'

The door swung open slowly and Watson's bulky form appeared on the threshold. The tubby lawman glanced anxiously around as if expecting an ambush.

'You can trust me,' Morgan said, 'They've quit town.'

Watson looked down at the body of Col McCool and then swiftly away again. 'What happened to him?' he asked.

'The outlaws used him to send us a message,' Bishop replied grimly. 'They carried off Miss Persimmon. They propose to trade her for the prisoner.' He nodded towards the door of the sheriff's office. 'I don't care to bargain with such men. Though given the circumstances I fear we have little choice.'

'Well now, well now,' Watson said nervously. He looked at Morgan, then at Bishop, then down at the corpse. 'Now you see, you see,' he said, looking up at Morgan again, 'now you see, this is where, this is where you might have hit a snag.'

'What do you mean, a *snag?*' Morgan asked.

'Well, see,' the sheriff said, 'now, you can't go blaming that boy. No sir, you can't do that.'

'I'd be grateful if you would speed to your point, Sheriff,' Bishop said. His manner was as polite as ever but his eyes were fixed on the town's law enforcer and they were not friendly.

'The prisoner,' the sheriff said, avoiding looking at Bishop and addressing his remarks to Morgan, 'He made a grab for my boy's . . . the deputy's gun. All that shooting was going on. They was trying to cut through the roof. Lead flying every which way. The prisoner, he got a hold of that boy's pistol and dang if the thing didn't just go off accidentally and now that boy ain't with us no more.'

'Which boy?' Morgan asked, though he had a sinking feeling he knew the answer.

'The prisoner,' Watson replied. 'My boy, it weren't his fault. That outlaw, he was trying to escape. That's the Lord's honest truth. I'll testify to that.'

'Sheriff Watson,' Bishop said, stepping up on to the sidewalk and staring hard at the rotund law officer, 'Are you telling me the prisoner I entrusted to your safe keeping is dead?'

Watson swallowed hard. 'Well, now . . . like I said — ' he continued.

Bishop cut him off abruptly. 'A simple yes or no will suffice, Sheriff,' he said.

Watson looked at Morgan, then at the ground. Then he nodded his head. 'Yes,' he mumbled.

Bishop took a deep breath. For a moment Morgan thought he might be about to smash a fist into Sheriff Watson's jutting waistband. Instead, the marshal exhaled slowly, shook his head, thought for a moment, and then said, 'Who knows about this?'

Watson shrugged nervously. 'I don't know. I mean, me, you, Mr Morgan there and my boy, I guess.'

'Nobody else?' Bishop asked pointedly.

'No, I guess not,' Watson replied.

'Well,' Bishop said, staring into the sheriff's round face, 'may I request we keep it that way? Because,' Bishop took a half-step forward and suddenly the revolver was in his hand, the barrel pointed up under the fat lawman's chin, 'if I should hear anybody else in this town so much as mention a dead prisoner, I will ensure they get another death to gossip about.' He tapped the barrel of his pistol on Watson's tin star of office. 'Is my meaning clear to you, Sheriff?'

'Yes . . . yes, sir, Marshal,' Watson stammered.

'Good,' Bishop said. 'Now, Mr Morgan and I are going into your office to converse with the deputy. I suggest you fill your time wisely by going across to the saloon and eating some pancakes.' Holstering his pistol deputy US marshal Bishop moved to enter the office.

Sheriff Watson did not budge, however. 'Now listen here,' he said, 'I won't have any harm done to my boy, you understand me?'

Bishop smiled slightly at this sudden unexpected show of courage. 'You have my word, Sheriff,' he said with his customary politeness. Then, as Watson stood to one side, he and Morgan entered the office of Lone Pine's lawman.

The smell of gunfire hung in the air and the floor was covered with sods of earth and plaster chippings brought down from the ceiling by the knife of the attackers and the sheriff's shooting. Plug Watson sat in the chair behind his father's desk. He was hunched over, rocking slowly back and forth, his head in his hands. In the jail cell the body of Billy Bearpaw lay on the floor, boot soles pointed towards the door.

The keys to the cell were on a large metal ring suspended from a hook above Plug Watson's head. Bishop took them and opened the cell door. Once inside he lifted up the corpse of the prisoner with a grunt of effort and placed it on the cot at the rear of the cell so that it faced the wall. He covered the body with a blanket. Anyone looking in from the street would assume Billy Bearpaw was asleep.

Bishop looked down at the floor of the cell. There was some blood on it but not much. Most of it must have soaked into the outlaw's clothing. The prisoner's blanket-coat and his high-crowned dark hat decorated with a beaded band and rooster feathers were laid out on a low bench near the wall. The lawman picked them up, slung the coat over his left arm and, holding the hat in his hand, stepped out of the cell and locked the door behind him.

While Bishop had been busy with Bearpaw's body Morgan had been trying to coax some sense out of the distraught Watson. Crouching with his arm around the boy's shoulders he assured him that nobody blamed him for what had happened.

'From what your daddy said it was all an accident,' Morgan said softly.

'That's right,' Plug replied. 'Only I should have known. You warned me, Mr Morgan, 'bout waving my gun around. You told me. Only I didn't listen. I'm a fool. And now that boy's dead.' He began to shudder again.

'Boy,' it was Bishop, 'you listen to

what I have to say. What occurred here was a mistake. Everybody can make a mistake. What we have to do as men is learn from our mistakes and make amends for them. Is that something you want to do?'

Plug Watson nodded his head eagerly. 'Yes, sir. I do.'

Bishop patted the boy on the shoulder. 'That's good,' he said. 'Now I'm going to tell you how you're going to do just that.'

* * *

Night had fallen and Longeye, Marat and the rest of the gang were back at camp. The yellow-haired woman was tied up in one of the log cabins. She'd refused to eat the food they'd offered. She'd get hungry soon enough. Then she'd beg for whatever they could spare. Marat chewed on a hunk of the dark mule flesh. Even though Two Birds had boiled it for several hours it was still tougher than belt leather.

'You figuring we got enough fire-power left to take on the Clergyman, *ami?*' Marat asked.

Longeye spat a chunk of gristle into the blazing fire and watched it sizzle. He took his time replying. 'Maybe,' he said eventually, 'Maybe not.'

'Well, that's set my mind at rest, *mon frère*,' Marat said with a laugh. 'You consider asking your cousin Little Crow to loan us a few of his braves?'

Longeye rose slowly from the pine log on which he was sitting, stretched his back and looked upward. The chill sky was clear again and the blackness above his head was speckled with thousands of stars. When he was a child his mother had told him that every twinkle of light in the heavens was the spirit of a brave warrior.

'One day, if you show courage and fight well you will join them,' she had said, 'but that day is a long time off.'

Watching the stars blinking down at him now Longeye felt that the day when he would be up there too was getting nearer. So near that he seemed almost to hear it coming, like the sound of horses galloping far off across the prairie. He had been brave and he had fought well. Soon he would look down from the darkness on other men like himself. If the white men had not killed them all.

'Do not worry,' he said to Marat. 'Youngbuck is at Little Crow's camp now. He will return tomorrow with more braves. Enough to kill the Clergyman and Crooked Hands.'

★   ★   ★

Morgan spent the next forty-eight hours preparing for the expedition into the Black Hills. He cleaned, oiled and loaded his weaponry, sharpened his Bowie knife till it was keen enough to cut paper. He bought provisions of beef jerky and pinto beans, molasses and coffee and filled a silver hip flask with the judge's finest Kentucky bourbon. Morgan's law student finances did not run to the keeping of a horse, but he had the pick of the Persimmon stable. Like many of his compatriots from the South, the judge had an abiding love and deep knowledge of horseflesh. Following his wise counsel Morgan plumped for a solid, soot-black gelding named Beauregard.

'Old Beau isn't as fast as he once was,' the judge said, stroking the white blaze on the beast's sleek forehead. 'But he's strong, sure-footed and slow to panic, and I guess for the situation you're heading into those virtues are of more value.'

Morgan would be taking along Kitty's dapple-grey filly, Louisa, too.

'I don't want to see this horse again unless my daughter's mounted on her,' the judge said to Morgan as he checked over Louisa's hoofs.

Morgan did not see Bishop again until the eve of their departure. He'd finished his dinner and was in his room making his final preparations when the widow called him down to the parlour.

The deputy US marshal was sitting by the stove in a button-backed velvet chair. An oiled canvas gun case was propped between his feet.

When the two men were settled Widow Jennings went off to make them fresh coffee. An awkward silence followed.

Eventually Morgan said, 'You sure about taking young Plug Watson with us?'

'I don't see that we have much choice,' Bishop replied. 'Longeye is expecting us to bring his nephew. Watson's the same age as Bearpaw and roughly his height and build. We dress him in the outlaw's coat and hat and Longeye is going to have to get pretty close to discern the difference.'

'How you figuring we should play the exchange?' Morgan enquired.

Bishop shrugged. 'I doubt Longeye is planning a trade. He's simply luring us into his territory with the intention of killing us both.'

'Is that what you really believe, or is

it just what you're hoping?' Morgan asked, a flinty note in his voice.

Bishop tilted his head slightly to one side. 'I don't fully understand your meaning, Mr Morgan,' he said evenly.

'Maybe it's you who's planning to kill rather than trade,' Morgan said, a glint of anger in his voice. 'Bishop, you have no concern for the life of Miss Persimmon. All you want is to put a bullet in Longeye's head.'

'I have made no secret of that fact,' Bishop responded in his courteous manner. 'But believe me, Mr Morgan, you'd be far safer placing yourself between a female grizzly bear and her cubs than staking your life on the good intentions of Louis Longeye. You saw what he did to that poor Irishman — and I doubt that fellow ever once pointed a gun at them and threatened to shoot.'

Morgan was about to respond when the door to the parlour opened and the Widow Jennings came back into the room with a tray. She poured them both a cup of dark coffee, advised them to try some of her buttermilk cookies, and then announced that she was going to pay a visit on the judge. 'That poor man may benefit from some home cooking,' she said with a kindly smile.

The widow's appearance and the mention of the judge afforded Morgan the chance to take a deep breath and step back from what had looked like developing into another fierce argument. He determined to remain on cordial terms with Bishop. As Judge Persimmon had counselled, hostility between the two men was of no benefit to anybody save the outlaws.

After the widow had gone off to ready herself for visiting Morgan raised a hand, as if to acknowledge that he had spoken too aggressively. 'How many men do you figure Longeye has with him now?' he asked.

'I'd reckon there's Marat and maybe three or four others,' Bishop replied. His own tone remained unaltered.

Morgan shrugged. 'Well,' he said, 'that doesn't seem such bad odds given you shot five of them at the last encounter.'

Bishop allowed himself a faint smile. 'I'd certainly share your optimism, Mr Morgan, if only that prisoner hadn't been killed. That has *complicated* the situation.' The deputy US marshal fingered the gun case, the butt end of which rested between his feet. 'What weaponry are you planning on packing, Mr Morgan?'

Morgan replied that he had a revolver, a sawn-off scattergun and the pepperbox pistol.

'All three are fine for close-quarters work,' Bishop said, 'but up in the Black Hills you're going to need something with more range to it.'

Morgan raised his hands ruefully. 'I can't work a Winchester rifle,' he said. 'These fingers of mine can't get a hold on the pump mechanism.'

'That's what I calculated,' the marshal said, 'which is what made me think of this.'

Bishop placed the gun case on the

widow's floral rug and flicked off the catches. From it he removed a 28-inch-barrelled gun with a polished oak stock. He held the rifle up for Morgan to inspect.

The other man looked at it and smiled. 'It's got a cylinder,' he said with a hint of surprise.

Bishop nodded, 'Remington .44 Army model revolving carbine,' he said. 'Company made less than a thousand of them. Couldn't compete with the Winchester for popularity, but for a man . . . ' he paused briefly looking for the right word, '*afflicted* as you are, it might prove ideal. The cylinder action is just like that on a pistol. No need to pump anything. Of course, it only holds six bullets to the Winchester's seventeen, but in my experience it's a good deal less likely to jam, and easier to free up if it does. I can cut off the trigger guard easily enough.'

Bishop handed the carbine to Morgan, who turned it over in his hands inspecting the polished steel of the firing mechanism. Noticing some markings on the barrel he said, 'You use this in the war?'

Bishop smiled. 'Once or twice,' he said.

Morgan glanced up from the gun. 'I served in the First Minnesota Volunteers under Major-General Hancock,' he said. 'Survived Gettysburg, though I sometimes wonder how. Eight out of every ten of us were killed or wounded. Major-general said later he was surprised it wasn't more. He expected *all* of us to die.'

'Is that where you damaged your hands?' Bishop asked.

Morgan shook his head. 'Nope,' he said. 'Nature achieved what man could not. A snowstorm did this to me. In Kansas.' He studied Bishop for a moment. 'I'm guessing from that hat of yours we were on opposite sides,' he said.

'You are correct,' Bishop said. 'I served in the Confederate Cavalry.'

'With Stuart?' Morgan asked.

Bishop shook his head. 'No,' he said,

'not with J.E.B. Stuart ... ' The marshal had been relaxed when discussing the carbine, but now Morgan noticed that he had become more watchful. His body suddenly alert. 'The unit I rode with,' Bishop continued, 'was less *formal* in nature.' He looked at Morgan, who saw that a hardness had returned to the marshal's eyes.

'You rode with Quantrill?' Morgan asked.

Bishop looked Morgan straight in the eye. '*Captain* Quantrill was gone by the time I joined them. I rode with Bill Anderson, and when he was killed, Archie Clement.'

Morgan was silent. Even during those violent times Anderson and Clement stood out. The Confederate bushwhackers were brutal and murderous. During raids into Union territory they butchered women and children. When Northern soldiers captured or killed them they found scalps in their saddle-bags. After the war finished most of Anderson's men carried on as if the surrender had never been signed. The James-Younger gang were still on the loose robbing banks and trains.

Bishop rose from his chair. 'The past is done. We have a common enemy now, Mr Morgan,' he said and reached out his right hand. Morgan looked at it, but did not take it.

The marshal sighed. 'See here, Mr Morgan. I do not need a partner, and even if I did it is plain you would not apply for the job. These are the cards we have been dealt and we must play them, whether we like them, or not.' He stretched his right hand out again. After a brief hesitation Morgan took it.

'Thanks for the rifle,' he said. 'I appreciate it.'

Ambrose Bishop nodded. 'We had better get some rest,' he said. 'We leave at first light tomorrow. I only hope the snow will hold off.'

Morgan shuddered slightly even though the parlour was warm. 'You and me both,' he murmured.

6

They set off a couple of hours before dawn. Even at this hour Lone Pine's main street was busy. Bearded, grim-faced prospectors trudged off towards the darkness of the foothills tugging at reluctant mules; the empty flatbed wagons of the lumber men rattled over the hard-frozen earth and the steam-powered machinery of the sawmill snarled and hissed, filling the grey, moonlit air with the scent of fresh-cut timber. A couple of stockmen were channelling longhorn steers down the alley by The Dutchman's saloon to the auction pens beyond. Inside The Dutchman's the oil lamps burned for the benefit of customers who were drinking late or starting early.

Bishop and Morgan flanked young Watson, who wore the outlaw's buffalo-hide coat and hat. His fur collar was pulled high, his hat brim tugged low, and a dark woollen muffler obscured most of the rest of his face. Plug straddled his father's horse, a barrel-flanked bay mare named Betsy, who was as amiable, slow-moving and fond of chow as her owner. At Bishop's insistence the young man's hands had been tied, though loosely. The deputy US marshal said the precaution was for the benefit of prying eyes, though Morgan couldn't help wondering if it was actually a measure to prevent the nervy juvenile creating more havoc with his shiny Colt six-shooter.

Bishop rode on the right of the group, astride a powerful, chestnut-coloured Tennessee pacer that stood seventeen hands at the withers, fully justifying his name: Samson. On Bishop's burnished leather saddle were mounted twin rifle scabbards, the one on the right holding a brass-framed Winchester .44–40, that on the left the lethal buffalo gun. The marshal's Remington revolver was housed in a saddle holster located behind the Winchester scabbard. A hornbag on the opposite side was stocked with ammunition for the rifles. Shells for the pistol were in the gunbelt around Bishop's waist. A pair of twin-buckled saddle-bags, one featuring a scabbard bearing a horn-handled knife, and an oilcloth covered blanket roll completed the lawman's baggage.

Morgan, wearing a thick, tan canvas coat with a broad shearling collar, rode on Watson's left, Louisa, the dapple-grey, trotting nimbly behind the dark bulk of old Beau. The new revolving rifle was in a scabbard on the front left, the rest of Morgan's weaponry housed in the customized gunbelt around his waist. At the last minute he had elected to tuck the pepperbox pistol into one of his saddle-bags. It seemed unlikely to be useful where they were heading, but Morgan had come to regard the small, ungainly looking gun as a lucky charm. A silver flask filled with the judge's best Kentucky bourbon was tucked in alongside it. Morgan's blanket roll contained one of Kitty's heaviest winter coats. The young woman had been wearing a house dress when she was abducted. Dying of exposure was one of the many perils she currently faced.

They rode north, through the mine workings and the tent city of the forty-niners. Camp fires glowed in the darkness, bleary-eyed, pale-cheeked men clustered around, warming their hands and coughing up pit dust from raw lungs. After half an hour horse hoofs crunched through the sheet ice of a wide, shallow stream. Spiders' webs covered in frozen dew hung from the bankside ferns like diamond necklaces. Soon after the crossing they began to ascend into the forest. Tall hardwood trees and wide evergreens, their branches silvered with frost, cast spindly moon-shadows across the dark trail.

They had not gone far into the woodland when Bishop held up his hand for them to halt. Drawing his Winchester from its scabbard, the marshal dismounted and, motioning for them to wait, moved off in a low crouch into the underbrush to his right. He returned holding the bloody remnants of what had once been a plaid shirt.

'This must be the place they captured that Irishman,' he said sombrely. The memory of the gory face of the unfortunate prospector sent a tingle of apprehension through Morgan. Instinctively he reached forward and rested his hand on the polished stock of his rifle. The Irishman's wounds were the mark of the men whose territory they were now riding into. If they dropped their guard for an instant they would likely suffer a similar blood-sodden fate.

The trio had ridden for more than an hour before the sun eventually rose above the eastern ridges and brought some warmth to their chilled bones. Near a trickling waterfall in a clearing of soft moss made rocklike by the cold they paused to brew coffee. Sheriff Watson had provisioned his son with a dozen fresh griddlecakes wrapped in wax paper. The trio ate them greedily.

The food clearly cheered Watson. The youngster had been silent throughout the ride, his cheeks pale under the shadow of the hat brim; now he spoke.

'I wanted to say, Marshal Bishop, how grateful I am for this chance to redeem myself. I know I fouled up, but I intend to put that behind me. One day I want to be a lawman just like my daddy.'

Bishop looked at the youngster. 'Well, now, son,' he replied evenly, 'I'd say there was every chance of you becoming a lawman exactly like your daddy.'

The irony of the marshal's meaning was lost completely on the boy. Blushing with pride he thanked Bishop for his kind words.

'That sure does mean a lot to me, sir,' he said. His sincerity was so patent that Morgan winced at it and, reaching across, patted the boy on the arm.

Bishop poured out the last of the coffee, then began to outline their situation.

'We're about four hours' ride from

the rendezvous with the outlaws,' he said, 'but we'll be in Longeye's territory a good deal sooner. From now on I think we may assume the hostiles are watching our every move. Son,' he said, gesturing to Watson, 'you keep that hat pulled down and the scarf up around your mouth. The longer the miscreants think you're Bearpaw the safer for all of us. Mr Morgan, you and I need to keep our ears pricked, our eyes skinned and our wits sharp. Should anything arouse your suspicion, no matter how trivial, you raise your hand. Anything at all. From now on there's no such thing as too cautious.'

Morgan nodded. 'You reckon they'll attack before we reach the river?' he asked.

Bishop shrugged. 'Maybe. Maybe not. The man we're dealing with,' he said, 'the only thing I can categorically rule out is a peaceful ending.'

A dozen miles after their break the riders crested a small ridge and found themselves looking across a high flat valley of soft pale grass, flanked by stands of cottonwood, spruce and pine. Peering ahead, Morgan raised his hand. The trio halted.

'You see something?' Bishop hissed.

'Up ahead,' Morgan replied quietly, pointing to something a mile off. 'Middle distance.'

Bishop took a pair of army field glasses from the pocket of his heavy woollen cape-coat. He studied the area Morgan had indicated.

'It appears the Irishman wasn't the only poor creature to encounter our friends recently,' he said. 'It's an abandoned prairie schooner. We'll go on, slowly, Keep an eye on those trees to the right and left. The folks riding in that wagon were ambushed, and I'd guess that's where it was sprung from.'

The trio moved towards what Morgan soon came to see was the wreckage of a homesteaders' four-wheeled wagon. It was one of the big ones that would carry a family and all their earthly possessions to a new life. If fate allowed them one. The pale canvas cover of the prairie schooner had been slashed and tatters of it hung forlornly around the iron bands that had once formed the roof-frame. The attackers had picked the wagon clean of anything usable, leaving the unwanted debris of the owners' lives to scatter in the wind.

They rode closer. The air was still. The valley was utterly silent save for the sound of the horses' breathing and the rattle of their metal shoes on the solid ground. Suddenly Watson's mare raised her head and whinnied nervously. Her hoofs noisily stamping, she sidestepped into Bishop's mount, bumping her muzzle against the big stallion's shoulder. As Plug struggled to stay in the saddle, he raised his head. As he did so something caught his eye. Lifting his bound hands from the horn of his saddle he pointed.

'Look, look,' he croaked in terror.

Morgan followed the boy's gaze. There was something moving in the bed of the wagon. He saw dark hair.

Bishop had seen it too. He reached out with his left hand to grab the bridle of Watson's shying mare, and with the other drew his Remington revolver. He fired once into the air, the report echoing out across the countryside. The movement in the wagon bed stopped momentarily. Then a dark shape reared up and stared at them for a split second before leaping from the side of the cart and bounding off towards the trees.

Watson's horse squealed in terror and would likely have spun and bucked her rider had Bishop's powerful grip not held her close to the side of his own, steadier mount.

'Darn it, what was that?' Watson grunted as he struggled to stay in the saddle, his bound hands gripping the mare's mane.

'A wolverine,' Bishop said, reholstering his revolver. 'As well you spotted it, son. It's not the biggest of God's creations, but it is surely one of the nastiest. Full grown male like that fellow can bring down an elk. It certainly might have done harm to one of the horses had we come up on him unexpectedly.'

'W-What was it doing in the wagon, Marshal?' Plug stammered nervously. Betsy had calmed again now the scent of the wolverine was no longer in her nostrils, but her eyes still flickered nervously and her rider remained unsettled.

Bishop exhaled, his breath smoky. 'The wolverine can hunt as well as any animal. He's lazy though. He likes to let others do the work for him. Then he feeds on the left-overs.' The lawman glanced across at Morgan, who saw that the marshal's face wore a grim aspect. 'I suspect you might hang back here with Mr Morgan, son,' he told Plug, 'And let me go and take a look in that wagon by myself.'

* * *

Henry Youngbuck and Pierre Gazon were out hunting. The pair were in an anxious frame of mind. Longeye had questioned them again about what had happened at the jail. He just didn't seem to believe that one man could have held off the five of them. Yet that same man had dispatched the three other members of the gang Longeye had sent to kill him. Got the best of them, even though they had surprise on their side. They had failed too, but they were dead, so all of Longeye's unhappiness was directed at Henri and Jean. And Longeye's unhappiness with people tended to last only a short time, for him and for them.

The two young outlaws were gloomily trailing a herd of pronghorn antelope when they heard the pistol shot. The pair started running the moment they heard it, covering the ground in agile leaps. Their ponies were tethered a hundred yards away amongst a group of aspens; they reached them quickly, swung effortlessly on to the bare backs of their mounts and were soon cantering in the direction of the noise. They rode side by side, talking as they went.

'It came from the place where we took the family two moons ago. It must be the Clergyman and Crooked Hands. Louis sent that young Lakota brave, Eagle Tail to watch them. Maybe they saw him. Maybe he's dead.'

They soon learned the last of these surmises was not the case. Eagle Tail was crouched behind some tall grey rocks. He was dressed in buckskin britches, decorated with wide black bands and a grey coat made from a trade blanket. His face was a mask of red and black war paint. His hair, worn in long plaits, was topped with a roach of hardened porcupine hide, decorated with two wild-turkey feathers.

Eagle Tail's pinto pony was tethered near by. Youngbuck had brought Eagle Tail and ten other Lakota warriors to Longeye's camp the day before. Eagle Tail was the son of the Lakota chief, Little Crow, and was considered the best tracker and hunter amongst his people. It was said he walked so quietly and ran so swiftly he could come up behind a bear, tap it on the back and disappear again before it turned round. They said the same thing about Louis Longeye.

Eagle Tail heard the riders approaching and turned swiftly, single-shot Starr carbine raised to his shoulder. When he saw who it was he lowered the barrel. He gestured for them to come forward more quietly, indicating that the enemy was near by. Youngbuck and Gazon slipped from their ponies and walked towards him, leading their mounts by their rope halters. They tethered them near to Eagle Tail's horse and, bent almost double, trotted to join the Lakota brave in his concealed position behind the boulders.

'The two men and Bearpaw,' Eagle Tail whispered. 'They just scared off a wolverine.'

'Mind if I take a peek?' Youngblood asked. All three of the men were tucked down behind the rocks, completely out of sight of Bishop, Morgan and their 'prisoner'.

'All right. But be careful,' Eagle Tail

said. 'I've followed them since sunup. They are vigilant.'

'You think they seen you?' Gazon asked.

Eagle Tail shook his head. 'No. But they are suspicious. They know they will be watched.'

Youngblood slowly lifted his head until his eyes were above the rock. Looking across the flat grassland he could see the Clergyman inspecting the contents of the wagon — the remains of a family of German settlers whose pale scalps were now drying on the lodge-pole of Longeye's cabin. Beyond the wagon sat the one Marat and Longeye called Crooked Hands, and with him, slumped forward in his saddle, was Billy Bearpaw.

A thought formed in Youngblood's mind. He ducked back behind the rock.

'We could take them,' he said.

Eagle Tail shook his head. 'Longeye told me only to follow. We will attack later with all our braves.'

'I know what he said,' Youngbuck

replied. 'But look see, Longeye's mad with me and Jean here. Sent us to break out Billy from Lone Pine jail, only we couldn't do it. Got ourselves bush-whacked by that Clergyman. Killed just about everyone but us two. So now Louis's acting like we should have stopped in town and got ourselves shot too. Wouldn't have made no difference. But that's the way he sees it. Blames us. Am I right, Pierre?'

Gazon nodded. 'When Louis's mad at you it's dangerous to sleep,' he said glumly.

'Way I figure it,' Youngblood said, 'if we can get Billy back and kill those two lawmen into the bargain, then Louis's not going to be mad with us no more and we can rest easy.'

'If this Clergyman killed so many of your people before why will it be different this time?' Eagle Tail asked.

'Because this time we got surprise on our side,' Youngblood said. 'Got my hunting rifle here,' he slapped the polished stock of the long-barrelled flintlock musket he was carrying, 'and Jean got his. We can pick them two Yankees before they even know we're here.'

Eagle Tail looked at Youngblood. 'I am not sure. Longeye said — '

'Listen up,' Youngblood snapped. 'You want to be part of this, then we all share the glory. You don't, then you'd better go someplace else, because me and Pierre ain't going to sit around waiting for Longeye to come cut our throats.'

Eagle Tail thought for a moment, then nodded. 'All right,' he said, 'we do it.'

* * *

Bishop did not look long at what the wolverine had been feasting on in the wagon bed. He had expected it to be gruesome and it was. Four more victims of Louis Longeye's personal war against the white men, two of them barely old enough for school. Mercifully the gang had been in a hurry. The dead family had not suffered long, though even that was long enough. Bishop rubbed his eyelids, cleared his throat and turned his stallion back towards the others. Morgan saw the expression on his face and knew better than to ask what he had just seen. Plug Watson was not so sensitive.

'What was it, Marshal?' he asked. 'What was that critter feeding on?'

Bishop shook his head. 'Nothing I'd care to describe,' he said. He glanced down at the belly of Watson's mare. 'Now look there,' he said. 'When Betsy shied just now her cinch came loose. You keep her steady and I'll tighten it up.'

Bishop leaned down low to grasp buckle and leather. As he did so he heard something whistle above his head. The sound was followed swiftly by the crack of a rifle. When he looked up Plug Watson was no longer sitting astride Betsy.

'Ambush!' Morgan yelled. He flipped

open his coat and whipped the customised Smith & Wesson revolver from his gunbelt. He fired several shots in the direction of a cluster of boulders a hundred yards across the meadow, then jumped down from Beau to tend to Plug.

The boy was lying in a crumpled heap. As Morgan's boots hit the ground there was another crack of gunfire. A rifle ball slapped against the reinforced leather pommel of his saddle and ricocheted downwards, cutting a shallow groove along Beau's shoulder. The black gelding reared up in pain and terror and then sped off, with Louisa the dapple grey trailing in his wake.

'We'll get them later,' Bishop shouted as the two horses galloped away from the gunfire. He had caught the reins of Watson's mount, wrapped them around his forearm and was crouching down behind Samson, trying to get a fix on where the shots had come from. The white puffs of smoke from the outlaws' flintlock muskets made that simple enough. Bishop raised his Winchester and let fly, lead smacking into rock with an angry snarl.

'How's the boy doing?' the deputy US marshal called out as he paused to see what reaction his shooting produced.

Morgan was kneeling beside the prone form of Watson. The rifle shot had been aimed at the back of Bishop's head. Instead it had struck the young deputy square in the heart. He was pale and his eyes were closed. He had been dead before he hit the ground.

'We lost him,' Morgan barked back.

Bishop fired another clutch of shots at the rocks up ahead.

'All right,' he called. 'Sling the boy over his horse and let's get out of here. Those fellows have Plains long rifles. Accurate, but a devil to reload, especially when you're lying down. I figure we have a minute or so at our disposal.'

As Morgan heaved the body of young Plug Watson on to Betsy, Bishop fired another burst of shots at the grey boulders. Glancing around and seeing that Morgan was now in the saddle, he sent a further cluster of bullets smacking into the outlaws' cover, then swung himself on to Samson, turned the big stallion, and came alongside Morgan. He pointed to a stand of pines some fifty yards away.

'Head for the trees,' he yelled. 'I reckon we should make it before they get off another shot.'

The riders rode hell for leather towards the grove, bending low over the polls of their horses. Betsy was nowhere near as quick as the marshal's powerful horse and, though the distance to cover was short, Morgan was still ten yards adrift of cover when the next rifle shot cracked out. The ex-lawman felt the bullet as it fizzed over his head and then he was in amongst the densely packed pines. Needle-coated branches smacked into his face and dislodged his Stetson, but he was through the trees soon enough. Up ahead the land fell away and he saw Bishop. The marshal was riding down towards a river. A wide bend carried water away to the east. The floods of the previous spring had undercut the steep banks, causing a number of tall ponderosa pines to collapse across it. The trunks and root-balls formed a natural stockade.

Bishop pulled his horse to a halt and turned and looked for Morgan. Seeing him coming on and evidently unharmed, he pointed to the cluster of fallen trees.

'If we have to make a stand,' he called, 'yonder looks as good a place as any we could have made for ourselves.' So saying he urged the big stallion forward again. Morgan followed and soon the two men had dismounted in what looked set to become their own little fortress.

'The bend in the river affords us protection on the right,' Bishop said, surveying the situation quickly and with his characteristic cool logic, 'The timber covers us on two sides. The only place we're vulnerable is to our rear.' He pointed back to the river, which was twenty yards across, deep and fast-flowing enough to deter a man on foot. 'Luckily there's enough melt water coming down from higher up to discourage anybody from attempting that route. I can't promise it's going to be cosy, Mr Morgan, but it will at least be safe. Take the boy's body and prop it against the tree stump there. We need to persuade them he's only wounded.'

Morgan stared at him, pricked once again by the marshal's unemotional response to events.

'Plug Watson is dead,' he said.

Bishop looked at him. 'I am aware of that, Mr Morgan,' he said. 'There are practical matters to attend if we are not to join him. The men who shot at us will be here soon enough. We have guns to reload and — '

'The bullet that killed him was meant for you,' Morgan said bluntly.

'Indeed,' Bishop replied. 'And I consider myself extremely fortunate I bent down when I did.' He looked at Morgan. 'And you should be, too.'

'And how do you figure that?' Morgan asked, his face flushing with anger.

'Put your feelings aside for a moment, Mr Morgan,' Bishop responded evenly, 'and ask yourself this. If that bullet had killed me instead of young Watson do you think the odds on your own survival would have shortened or lengthened?'

'Damn it, Bishop,' Morgan hissed. 'All I'm asking is for some sign of human feeling. A young boy just got killed. One you were joshing with about his daddy not twenty minutes ago. He wouldn't even have been here if we hadn't brought him. That doesn't seem to mean spit to you. Don't you feel any responsibility?'

Bishop was about to respond when the argument was interrupted by the sound of a whinnying horse.

7

Henri Youngbuck had watched in disbelief as the marshal's last minute duck of the head allowed his bullet to miss the intended target and hit what he believed was Billy Bearpaw instead. When Pierre Gazon failed to bring down Crooked Hands the young outlaws' bold attempt to redeem themselves in the eyes of Louis Longeye had become a debacle.

'What if Billy's dead?' Jean asked after his second shot had again failed to bring down Crooked Hands. 'Louis finds out you shot him, Henri, it's going to be bad, real bad.'

That was something Youngbuck did not need telling.

'Maybe Billy's just winged,' he said hopefully.

Eagle Tail shook his head glumly. 'He fell like a dead man,' he said.

Youngbuck stared at the ground, thinking: *We got to get the other two — the Clergyman and Crooked Hands.* He said, 'We kill them, then tell Louis they shot Billy. Say he tried to escape and they gunned him down. Say we saw it happen. Tell him we was watching, just like he told us. Then Billy bust loose and was galloping off and the Clergyman took out that big old buffalo gun and — bang! And when we saw that we went out for revenge.' He glanced at his two companions. 'We can do that,' he said.

Eagle Tail did not answer, but Gazon stroked the dark bristles on his chin and replied,

'Don't like it much, but I can't see as there's any other route we can take. We tell the truth, Longeye gonna kill us anyhow.'

Eagle Tail shrugged. He wished he had not listened to the whitemen in the first place. Now he had no choice but to follow them.

The three young men mounted their

ponies and rode off towards the wrecked prairie schooner. They saw the fresh blood on the ground where Watson had fallen and followed the hoofprints of the horses towards the pines. As they got closer to the trees they fanned out, Gazon and Eagle Tail circling to the right and left, while Youngbuck went straight ahead. When he came to the trees he dismounted and, carrying his long rifle in one hand, led his horse into the thicket of pines.

He paused when he came across Morgan's hat, but then pressed on. The pattern of the hoofprints indicated that the horses had been moving fast. It did not look like the riders had stopped in the trees. Sure enough, when he pushed through the branches of the final row of pines he saw empty ground sloping away, the fugitives' trail running down it towards a river. Gazon and Eagle Tail came into view to his right and left; both were astride their horses. When Gazon's mount saw Youngbuck's pony it let out a neigh of recognition.

The trio converged.

'I reckon they're down by that river,' Youngbuck said. 'We leave the horses here, spread out and try and get a fix on them.'

The others nodded. They hobbled the ponies and, carrying their guns split off as they'd done when approaching the pines. Youngbuck loped forward, bent low at the waist, head down, his rifle butt trailing almost to the ground. He had gone thirty yards when a glint of steel amidst a cluster of fallen trees alerted him to the presence of Morgan and Bishop. He hit the ground immediately and moments later a heavy calibre bullet fizzed a couple of feet over his head. Pulling his rifle into position he lifted himself on to his left elbow and sighted down the long barrel of the hunting gun seeking for a target.

★　★　★

Bishop slotted another shell into the Sharps rifle. He saved the Winchester for close quarters work or for when the situation demanded volume rather than precision. A shot rang out to his left and slapped into the trunk of the big ponderosa pine behind which Morgan had taken up position. Bishop could tell from the sound of the report that it wasn't a long rifle. It sounded like some sort of smooth-bore cavalry carbine. That meant there were three of them — the two men with the hunting guns and this fellow. In Bishop's experience woodsmen always carried the most accurate rifle they could. That meant the third member of the group wasn't a Metis. Most likely he was a full-blood Indian.

The Lakota didn't think much of guns. They preferred to fight face to face with knife or tomahawk. They bought cheap weapons from traders, old flintlocks and percussion cap carbines left over from the Civil War. That wouldn't have been so bad if they looked after them properly, but they didn't. They cut off the back sights and loaded the guns with pebbles when they ran out of rifle balls.

'There are three of them,' Bishop called out to Morgan. 'The fellow who just shot at you is poorly armed. He's going to have to get in close if he wants to hit anything. The other two have the long rifles and, I'd surmise, a fair idea how to use them. One of them is straight ahead of me. I'd guess the other is a way over to the right.

There was a crack, and a rifle ball slapped into the soft mud of the riverbank a couple of feet from Bishop, spraying his face with fine dirt.

'That will be him. It's as I thought,' he said. The tone of his voice gave no indication that he was locked in a battle for survival against a hostile foe. 'I'll wager your man is a Lakota. Have you caught sight of him?'

Morgan stared through the foot wide gap between the underside of the fallen tree and the top of the riverbank. The Remington revolving rifle was at his shoulder. The marshal's cool calculation had aggravated him previously, but under fire he could see the value in it, admire it even.

'Not yet,' he shouted back. Then up ahead and slightly to his right he saw a figure with dark hair topped by black and white feathers scurry forward. 'You called it right,' he yelled to Bishop and squeezed off a shot that missed the advancing Indian by a couple of feet, but nevertheless sent him sprawling into the low cover provided by the undulating ground.

'That gun of his is more for noise than homicide,' Bishop shouted. 'He'll try and work his way forward so that he can rush you. The sooner you let him, the sooner he'll be dead.'

'Or I will be,' Morgan responded.

Morgan saw the turkey-feather headdress of the Indian appear again above the cover of a low grass covered ridge. The next second the Lakota brave was sprinting forwards towards a stand of small spruce trees. The former lawman fired off a shot. The bullet flew wide as the Indian darted behind the trees.

After a brief pause the Indian was off again, racing at a diagonal to the cover of a toppled cotton oak. Again Morgan's shot fizzed past the fleet-footed figure as he flung himself behind the gnarled trunk of the dead tree. He was crouching low but the feathers on top of his head protruded, betraying his position. It was these feathers Morgan fixed his eyes on as he used his thumb to check how many more rounds he had left in the cylinder of the revolving rifle: two.

Eagle Tail had been edging gradually closer to the man they called Crooked Hands. Every time he found fresh cover he made sure that his enemy saw the turkey feathers. Now that he was close enough he reached down to the belt round his waist and picked from it a pair of identical feathers. He attached them to a stick picked up from the ground. Ducking down so that his headdress disappeared momentarily from view Eagle Tail poked the stick into the dirt so that the feathers on it peeked up above the tree trunk. Satisfied with the result he began slowly to crawl away.

Morgan had been watching the turkey feathers for several minutes when it dawned on him that they had not moved for some while. Sighting the rifle on the larger of them he fired. The bullet took the tip of the feather clean off. Neither of the feathers moved in response. The law student barely had time to curse his own stupidity when he heard a bloodcurdling yell to his left. Swinging round he saw a Lakota brave in buckskins and full war paint charging towards him, triangular-bladed hatchet raised. The Indian was ten yards away and closing in fast.

Morgan considered turning the rifle on him, but the barrel was tucked into the gap between the riverbank and the fallen pine. Instead he stepped back a pace and reached for the sawed-off shotgun in his gunbelt, urging his crippled fingers to close on the wooden butt. As he withdrew the weapon he heard a whoop of triumph.

Looking up, he saw the Lakota leaping from the bank, right foot outstretched. The flying kick caught Morgan square in the chest knocking him backwards and down. His head struck the hard ground, stunning him and dislodging the sawed-off shotgun from his grip. As he turned hurriedly to grab for it, the Indian leapt on him. The brave's left hand pinned Morgan's throat, shoving his shoulders back to the ground. The Lakota's right arm was raised, the polished-steel edge of the hatchet glinting in the morning sun. Morgan watched as the tomahawk began its swift descent towards his face.

A shot boomed out behind him. The hatchet disappeared. The Indian shrieked as blood burst from a gaping wound in his shattered wrist. Another shot, this one from a pistol, hit the Lakota straight between the eyes, knocking him backwards.

Morgan turned on to his side, kicking his feet free of the dead redskin. Bishop had already reholstered his smoking pistol and was sliding a round into the breach of the Sharps rifle.

'There's no time to lie around, Mr Morgan,' he called, turning away from the man whose life he had just saved. 'I need you here on my right. These fellows are not brave, but since they believe they may have killed Louis Longeye's nephew they are indisputably desperate.'

★　★　★

On a bluff high above the outlaw camp Louis Longeye squatted on a rocky ledge and looked out across the forests, high valleys and sharp peaks of the Black Hills. In the sky to the east mounds of heavy clouds pregnant with snow moved slowly westwards. From the camp below came the occasional whoop of a Lakota brave. Marat had found whiskey in the wagon of the settlers they had ambushed. He had drunk until he passed out. Now the Indians had found what was left. Like all those who drank the whiteman's liquor they would become stupid, loud and clumsy. Longeye did not drink whiskey. He never had. He had seen too often what it did to people. Whiskey was like gold and so many other things the whitemen coveted. They thought it would make them happy, but instead it made them angry, violent and bitter.

Longeye was watching an eagle swooping low over tall pines when from far away he heard what he thought was a gunshot. He rose to his feet and stood silently, turning his head slowly, trying to pick up any noise. Youngbuck and his yellow friend, Gazon had gone hunting; perhaps it was them. He listened. A second shot and then a third, quieter this time, rang out, then a louder one. The last one Longeye recognized as coming from a long rifle. The quieter ones sounded like they came from a smaller-calibre, repeating gun. He turned his head again until he was facing south-east. A string of shots rang out from that direction. This was not the sound of hunting. It was a fight.

Longeye began to jog down the hillside to the camp. He was a big man and in his fifth decade but he moved with the nimble grace of a deer, hopping over rocks and dodging around trees and boulders as he skipped down the steep incline. He hit the level ground by the camp at a full trot. The sight of him coming seemed to sober the young Lakota warriors instantly. Marat, however, lay in a stupor by the glowing ashes of the campfire. The outlaw chief called for his men to mount up. The Indians found their ponies, so too did Jean Moosejaw, but Marat did not move. Longeye went over to him and stuck the toe of his moccasin into the man's ribs.

'Izzat?' Marat mumbled.

Longeye looked down at his friend. As usual his face betrayed no emotion, and when he spoke he said simply, 'There is too much white in you, Jacques.' Then he turned and went off to get his horse.

Marat, who had not responded to this comment, lay still. He appeared to be asleep but anyone examining him closely would have seen that he had one eye open and a faint, drunken grin on his face.

Longeye pulled himself on to his pony. The rest of his men were grouped around him.

'To the south-east, half-an-hour ride. There is a gun-fight. Must be the Clergyman and Crooked Hands. Eagle Tail, Youngbuck and Gazon are there.' He swung his horse round in the direction from which the firing had come and kicked it into a canter. The rest of his band followed, the Lakota yelping with excitement at the prospect of the bloodshed to come.

* * *

Morgan rested the barrel of the revolving rifle on the lip of the high bank that protected the right side of Bishop and his own position. He had succeeded in reloading the Remington and was now staring out across the bumpy ground that sloped towards the river. It was grassy water meadow, only the occasional boulder or low shrub offered any kind of cover for the enemy. Behind the ex-lawman Bishop stood alert and silent, squinting through the sight of the Sharps rifle. The air was freezing but if he was cold Bishop did not show it. Every muscle and sinew was concentrated on aiming his gun, on detecting the slightest movement that should offer him the chance to use it.

Ten minutes earlier Bishop had told Morgan, 'These boys are running out of time. Longeye must have heard our little exchange and he'll be on his way. Their only hope is to kill us before he gets here. To do that they're going to have to take a risk. Keep your wits about you and your gun ready. They'll show themselves soon enough.' The two men had not spoken since.

Morgan watched a low cluster of rocks seventy-five yards away to his front. He was not certain that the outlaw was behind it, but there was no other obvious place for him to shelter. He wondered how much longer he could keep this up. His knuckles were aching and his right shoulder had begun to cramp. The cold was gnawing at his flesh. He thought of the bourbon that had been in the saddle-bag of Beau and wondered where the judge's genial old horse had run to. The wound had been light. The elderly gelding would survive provided they could find him before either the outlaws or that wolverine did. And of course Kitty's mare, Louisa was with Beau.

The thought of the dapple grey's empty saddle brought a pang to Morgan's chest. In the battle for survival he had temporarily forgotten the reason he and Bishop were here. Pinned down by the river they were no nearer completing their mission than they'd been that morning when they set off. In fact — with Watson dead — they were further from it than ever. Kitty Persimmon had been in the hands of Louis Longeye for two days. The thought of what might have become of her chilled Morgan's blood more surely than the icy mountain air. He had to get her back. But how?

Morgan's wandering train of thought was brought abruptly to a halt by the appearance of dark hair above the rocks to his front. Slowly the hair rose and a dirt-streaked face appeared, eyes narrowed. Morgan took a deep breath and slowly and gently swung the gun barrel until the head of the outlaw was in his sights. Equally slowly and gently he began to squeeze the trigger. The head disappeared again. Morgan exhaled loudly in frustration.

'Have patience, Mr Morgan,' a low voice from behind him counselled. 'The chance will come again.'

Morgan took another deep breath and began to count. He'd got to twenty-three when the hair and then the face reappeared, slightly to the left of where they had been previously. He resighted more quickly this time and fired. His aim wasn't true, but the .45 bullet struck the rock directly below Gazon's face, sending a shower of sharp granite splinters up into his eyes. The outlaw screamed with pain and instinctively rose slightly as he did so. Morgan needed no further invitation. His second round struck clean in the chest. Gazon lifted himself to his feet momentarily, then toppled backwards with a dying holler.

Morgan had barely grasped what had happened when Bishop's buffalo gun thundered out to his rear. He turned to find the deputy US marshal smiling at him with satisfaction.

'Fine work, Mr Morgan. Now, if you don't mind waiting here I'll go and see if I can't recover the other horses. One of them was carrying some rather good whiskey, as I recall.'

* * *

Longeye and his men rode fast along the flat ground of a high meadow. The hoofs of their ponies drummed on the hard frozen turf and steam rose from the flanks of the animals. There were eleven of them in all — nine of Little Crow's young warriors, Jean Moosejaw and the leader. The faces of the Lakotas were painted with ash and vermilion. Eagle and turkey feathers, ermine skins and deer tails hung from the roaches in their long black hair. The white patches on their pinto ponies were decorated with coloured hand-prints, zigzag stripes and horseshoe designs that showed the number of ponies each rider had snatched when raiding.

One or two of the warriors had old flintlock carbines dangling from leather thongs around the necks of their mounts, but most carried only stone-headed warclubs bound with rawhide, and bows. The bows were made from green ash. They were short, designed to be shot from horseback at running buffalo. The hickory wood arrows they shot were tipped with bone and sinew. At a range of up to twenty paces they could go straight through the trunk of a fir tree, or pierce the hide of a bison and find its heart. Beyond fifty paces they were no more effective than a thrown rock.

Above the thumping of the ponies' hoofs Longeye had already heard the unmistakable booming report of a buffalo gun. To kill the Clergyman the braves would need to get close to him. Some, maybe most of them, would die.

The party rode on. Up ahead the gunfire seemed to have ceased. The ponies' breath blew like mist in the still, cold air. The snow clouds rolled inexorably on towards them, gradually eating away at the pale blue sky. As they crested a low rise one of the Lakotas let out a whoop and pointed excitedly ahead. Longeye followed the line of the brave's jutting arm. Cantering away from them, along the edge of a grove of pine trees was a dark-clad figure on a chestnut stallion. The Clergyman. He was leading two horses and appeared oblivious to their presence.

Longeye had wanted to maintain the advantage of surprise, to cut the Clergyman off from Crooked Hands, who must be near by, guarding Billy Bearpaw. But when the Lakotas caught sight of the rider they began to yell out their war cries. One discharged his carbine into the air. Before the outlaw leader could stop them the warriors were galloping wildly in pursuit of their foe. He and Moosejaw had little option but to follow in their wake.

* * *

Bishop had ridden out in the direction of the ransacked wagon. He found the spot where the unfortunate Watson had met his end and from there easily tracked the two missing horses. Old Beau was a steady animal. His panic had not lasted long. The deputy US marshal found him and his companion, Louisa, about half a mile away, sheltered amongst a stand of aspens nibbling at some tussocks of ryegrass. The dapple grey still seemed edgy, stamping the ground and snorting when she saw him. Bishop dismounted and approached her slowly and calmly, talking in a low soothing voice as he did so. A few minutes later he had strung both animals to the back of Samson and was riding back to Morgan.

He had gone no more than 200 yards when he heard the commotion of the Indians to his rear. Turning in his saddle he saw Longeye's band galloping towards him across the silver-tinged meadow. They were 400-yards off, but closing fast. Hearing the whoops and yelps of the Lakotas, Louisa — still nervous despite Bishop's best efforts to calm her — shied. Rising on to her rear legs she kicked the air and whinnied. One of her hoofs struck old Beau on the left hip. The veteran horse let out a snort of pain and tried to distance himself from the grey, straining against his ties and causing the marshal's stallion to stagger slightly to his left.

Realizing that trying to keep both

animals was to risk losing both, Bishop drew the sharp, short-bladed knife from the sheath attached to his saddle-bag and swiftly cut Louisa loose. The dapple grey instantly whirled about and, blinded by fear, galloped straight towards the approaching war party, before sheering off to the right.

The departure of the nervous mare put a stop to Beau's tugging. With Samson now providing a stable platform, Bishop drew the Sharps rifle. The braves were 300 paces away. He raised the gun, sighted slightly above the warrior at the front of the pack and squeezed the trigger. The report rang in his ear and a split second later his human target clutched briefly at his throat and then fell sideways from his horse, causing the following riders to swerve suddenly to right and left to avoid his corpse.

Bishop chambered another round and raised the heavy octagonal barrel of the rifle again. By now, however, the implications of what they'd just witnessed had registered with the warriors. Most had never fought a white man before, or encountered a gun of such power and accuracy. They pulled up their ponies, hesitating about what they should do. The deputy US marshal was in no such state of confusion. Drawing a bead on the nearest of the braves, he inhaled, held his breath, waited for a second until his mount was perfectly still, then fired. Another of the Lakotas tumbled to the ground.

Longeye and Moosejaw had caught up with the milling group of Indians at the same moment as the second brave hit the floor. Reining his pony to a halt, the outlaw leader leapt swiftly to the ground, swinging his Hawken long rifle from across his shoulder as he did so. He pulled his pony round broadside to him and, using its croup as a rest, aimed down the three-feet long barrel of the gun. After firing his second shot and halting the Indian charge, Bishop had slid his buffalo rifle back into its scabbard and was now trotting south-eastwards. Longeye traced his movement with the muzzle of his own hunting weapon, and when he was certain of his shot he fired.

The .40 lead ball from the outlaw's rifle had travelled close to a quarter of a mile before it struck the deputy US marshal in the left side of his chest, nicking his arm en route. If it hadn't come all that way things might have been worse. As it was the heavy ball's effectiveness was further dulled by having passed through the thick dense wool of his coat sleeve twice, the body of the same garment and the flesh of his arm. His flannel shirt, undervest and skin and muscle also intervened before the bullet struck a rib. The bone cracked, but held. Bishop let out a gasp of pain and was almost knocked from his saddle by the force. The effect of the shot — Bishop thought, as he righted himself and kicked Samson into a gallop — was like being struck by an unexpected body punch from a bare-knuckle prizefighter. It hurt like the devil, but would not incapacitate him for long.

The marshal steered the chestnut stallion into the cover of the trees on his right. Dismounting with a snarl of pain, he drew the Winchester from the saddle holster and fired four quick shots at the outlaw band. The repeater was not nearly as accurate as the buffalo rifle, but one round clipped an Indian pony, causing it to rear and unseat its rider, and another creased the scalp of Moosejaw, who shrieked with anguish. The other two bullets flew close enough to give the men pursuing Bishop pause for thought. Kicking at their horses and whooping, they turned and retreated back up the slope. The marshal fired a couple more shots in their direction as encouragement, then, leading Samson, walked deeper into the trees.

* * *

Morgan had built a fire from the timber surrounding the fallen ponderosas. He had cut kindling and shavings, using the dead Lakota's axe, and that along with handfuls of dry pine needles had soon created a good enough blaze to sooth the aching joints of his fingers. He was out collecting the weapons of the dead outlaws when he heard the boom of Bishop's faithful buffalo gun echoing through the trees. He picked up the long rifle from the man he had killed and scampered back to the riverbank. He was settling into the position at the front of the makeshift fortress previously occupied by the deputy US marshal when the second report of the Sharps bellowed out from beyond the pine copse 400 yards or so from where he stood. The revolving rifle was in his hands as he scanned the tree line for signs of movement. A third shot rang out, this one from a different weapon, one that was being fired from further away.

Morgan kept his eyes fixed on the tree line. He knew somebody would appear at some point through the pines. Sure enough a few minutes later they did. Thankfully it was Bishop. The deputy US marshal was mounted and signalled with a wave of his hat to his companion. From the way he was sitting the big stallion, Morgan knew right away he'd been hit.

When Bishop had trotted his horse down into the hollow beneath the fallen trees Morgan helped him dismount.

'You're hurt,' he said. The marshal assured him it was nothing serious, 'But I shall have to carry out some minor repairs. Mr Morgan, if you could do me the service of taking the knife from the scabbard on my saddle-bag and heating the blade in the fire I'd consider it a service.'

Morgan did as he was asked, retrieving the sharp, short-bladed knife and placing the blade in the glowing ashes. When he turned around Bishop had removed his coat and, with a grimace of discomfort, was peeling back his shirt. Blood caked the lower left side of his torso, but had evidently stopped flowing. The marshal poked at a dark wound on his chest, his face twitching as he did so.

'It's as I thought,' he said calmly. 'The slug is lodged close to the surface. While that knife is sterilizing I'd be grateful if you'd share some of the judge's whiskey with me, Mr Morgan.'

Morgan went and retrieved the silver flask from bags strapped to the saddle of Beau. The solid old horse seemed unfazed by his recent adventures and snorted amiably when Morgan patted his heavy flank.

Returning to the fire he found Bishop squatting over it, twisting the knife blade in the flames. The marshal turned as he approached and reached up with his free hand for the flask. Morgan flipped the cap and handed it to him. Bishop thanked him with his customary courtesy. Even having a bullet lodged in him did not seem to alter his belief in the importance of good manners.

Bishop took a hefty drink of bourbon and, the moment he had swallowed it, removed the knife blade from the flame. With barely a pause for breath he cut a cross-shaped nick above the wound, then inserted the point of the knife into it. With a flick of his wrist the marshal dislodged the musket ball and watched it fall to the ground at his feet. Then with a growl of pain he placed the flat of the red-hot blade against the wound to cauterize it. The flesh smoked, and for the first time since Morgan had encountered him Bishop emitted a quiet curse. Having tossed the knife point downward into the turf by the fire, the marshal removed a handkerchief from his pocket, poured some of the whiskey on to it and pressed the soaked cloth to the wound.

'I'm reluctant to waste such fine Kentucky bourbon,' he said to Morgan with a faint smile. 'But I'll judge even that is preferable to gangrene.' So saying, he handed the flask back to his companion.

Morgan drank. 'So what happened?' he asked as he felt the liquid begin to burn warmly in his belly. Bishop related events as he pulled his coat back on.

'Longeye aside, they look a pretty raw

bunch,' he said as he finished. 'Young Lakota bucks mainly, and poorly armed. I put a fright into them, but that won't last long.'

'Where did they come from, the Indians?' Morgan asked.

'Longeye's cousin, Little Crow, is a Lakota chief.'

'You didn't mention we'd be fighting the Sioux when we set out,' Morgan said.

Bishop smiled, 'I didn't see the need to worry you,' he said.

Morgan laughed and took another swig of bourbon. 'Did Longeye have Miss Persimmon with him,' he asked hopefully.

Bishop shook his head. 'I'm afraid not. Marat wasn't there either,' he said. He patted the other man on the shoulder, then turned and walked to his horse. He drew both his rifles and took two cardboard cases of ammunition from a horn bag.

'We need to prepare ourselves, Mr Morgan,' he said in his characteristic even tone. 'We have resisted many perils today, but I fear the worst is yet to come.'

Morgan followed him to the front of their position. It seemed that if he was to rescue Kitty he would have to step over Longeye's corpse to do so.

8

Marat had waited until a few minutes after Louis Longeye and the others had left the camp before he raised his head. His brain clanged like a church bell on Easter Day and his mouth tasted as if a grizzly bear had been hibernating in it. He turned on to his side and slowly raised himself on to all fours. A wave of nausea rose in his stomach. He vomited on to the red and orange embers of the campfire, sending an evil-smelling smoke spiralling up into the clear blue sky. Damn that mule meat. He'd never eat that again. Wiping his mouth with the back of his hand Marat rose groggily to his feet and staggered over to his pony, which was tethered to a birch tree thirty feet away. He was sick twice more before he reached it.

He took a canteen from a loop on the saddle horn, unscrewed the cap and took a deep draught from it. The water inside was so cold it made him gasp and cough. The icy liquid set off further explosions inside his skull and he collapsed on to all fours, retching. He stayed like that for several minutes, stars flashing before his eyes. When finally he lifted his sore and aching head he found he was looking straight across the camp to the doorway of the log cabin in which the woman was imprisoned. Now he remembered why he had stayed behind and risked the wrath of his blood brother. The yellow-haired woman was pale as moonlight on snow, her eyes were blue and she smelled like a mountain meadow. However angry Longeye was she would surely be worth it.

Marat rose slowly to his feet. Taking the canteen he poured the freezing water over his head, wheezed and gulped, then shook himself dry like a dog. His head still throbbed and his stomach was turning somersaults. He needed more whiskey. He had some hidden in his wigwam. He would go and get that. Then he would make himself presentable and pay a call on the judge's daughter.

* * *

Kitty had heard the horses leaving and thought that perhaps she was alone in the camp. She was struggling to free herself from the leather thongs that bound her hands behind her back when she heard the sound of a man vomiting. The judge's daughter listened carefully after that. The man seemed to be alone and was apparently incapacitated by illness. The night before had plainly been one of heavy drinking. She had been woken by wild whoops and heard a rasping drunken voice singing in French about a girl he loved — a blonde girl, she realized now with a shudder of horror. She guessed the drunken singer was the evil, stinking villain who'd held her at knifepoint in her home and carried her here slung across his horse. It was this same silver-haired coward who'd brought her the revolting meal that lay untouched at her feet. He had looked at her the way a fox looks at a plump hen. It made her, squirm to think of the man. But perhaps, if she was alone with him, she could turn his predatory attentions to her advantage.

Looking around the cabin Kitty noticed that a series of bent hobnails had been banged into the log walls, from which to hang beaver and other pelts. Rising to her feet she went over and inspected them. The nails were square and their edges narrow. Turning her back to the wall the young woman moved her arms until the leather thong around her wrists hooked over one of the nails. Then she began to move her hands backwards and forwards. It took several minutes before the nail edge began to cut into the leather. Her arms aching with the effort, Kitty worked busily. She had begun to feel the binding give when she heard the knock on the cabin door.

'Wh-who is it?' she called out, desperately sawing at the leather.

'It is a gentleman calling for the mademoiselle,' replied a gruff voice she recognized as that of the silver-haired outlaw.

'Which gentleman?' Kitty asked, still working on her bindings and trying to keep the exertion out of her voice.

'Monsieur Jacques Marat,' the voice came back. It was thick with drink.

With one final effort Kitty succeeded in cutting the bonds. Her hands free, she brought them round to her front, massaging the red raw skin.

'Just one moment, *monsieur*,' she called. Quickly she surveyed the room for something to use as a weapon. The horrible meat had been brought to her in a heavy iron skillet. Emptying the vile contents on to the dirt floor, she propped the frying pan against the wall and then sat down in front of it, her hands behind her back. '*Entrez, monsieur*,' she called out.

The door opened and Marat stepped inside. He had plastered his wild hair down on his head with some sort of grease, and had evidently made an effort to wash his face. Or at least parts of it. As he stepped inside he grinned at her, flashing a gold tooth and many black ones.

'Ah,' he said, 'you are even lovelier than I remember, mam'selle.'

Even from several yards away the smell of the man was hideous, and his lascivious smirk turned Kitty's stomach, yet she replied sweetly,

'And you are so, so much more charming, *monsieur*.'

Marat chuckled. Even in his wildest dreams he had not imagined things would go this well with the yellow-haired woman. He had thought he would have to be rough with her. Perhaps she had enjoyed being kidnapped, thought it romantic. Who could tell with women?

'I don't suppose, *monsieur*,' Kitty enquired politely, 'that you might have any brandy or whiskey to' — she thought for a moment searching for the right words — 'warm my heart?' she said eventually. The woodsman grinned horribly, his leathery skin forming dimples and his grey eyes twinkling beneath filthy eyebrows.

'Why yes, I do,' he said. 'Should I fetch it?'

Kitty gave him her loveliest smile. 'That would be most agreeable, Monsieur Marat . . . Jacques,' she said. Marat made a gesture as if tipping his hat to her and scurried out of the door. As soon as he was gone Kitty picked up the heavy skillet and positioned herself next to the entrance of the cabin.

★   ★   ★

Once they were out of gunfire range Longeye rallied the Lakotas.

'The whiteman's gun fires far,' he said, 'but no gun can hit what it cannot see. From now on, brothers, we must hunt as the mountain lion, not as the wolf pack.'

The Metis outlaw divided the remaining braves into two groups of three and four; he sent the smaller one directly east with instructions to loop around by the ambushed wagon and follow the tracks of the Clergyman, Crooked Hands and their prisoner Billy Bearpaw. The larger group he sent south, telling them to turn east only when they reached the bank of the river they called the Snake Horn. He and Moosejaw would follow the Clergyman directly and find where he was hiding. The pincer movement would ensure that they would be unable to escape back to Lone Pine, or break through to Longeye's stronghold and rescue the woman. The Lakotas would rally to the leader at his signal — the birdcall repeated three times.

After the braves had galloped off, the two woodsmen dismounted and moved towards the trees into which Bishop had disappeared. They moved slowly, careful to keep their ponies between themselves and any enemy who was lurking out of sight in the pines. By this cautious method they zigzagged down the slope. It took them ten minutes to reach the grove of trees, another five to locate the spent shell cases from Bishop's Winchester.

'You think you hit him?' Moosejaw asked.

Longeye grunted and nodded his head. He had seen the Clergyman reel in the saddle after he fired. He knew his aim had been good.

'Maybe he'll bleed to death before we can find him,' Moosejaw said hopefully. Longeye did not answer. He had been looking for blood since they reached the place where the deputy US marshal had ridden into the firs. He could find none. Slowly they traced Bishop's tracks through the trees, pausing regularly to listen for sounds. They had stopped by a group of pale-trunked birches when Longeye's nostrils twitched.

'Wood smoke', he said. Turning his head from side to side the outlaw leader sniffed the air. 'A thousand paces from here,' he said, 'directly south.'

Moosejaw furrowed his tanned brow. 'That would put them right on the banks of the Snake Horn,' he said.

Longeye thought for a moment, then said, 'Yes, there is a place there that would be easy to defend. That is where the Clergyman will have gone.'

The two outlaws tethered the ponies. Taking their long rifles they began picking their way through the trees. When they reached the point where the pines gave way to open grassland the pair crouched down and gazed ahead. Smoke rose into the empty winter sky from an unseen fire. Beyond the smoke high ponderosa pines and Douglas firs formed a dark backdrop.

'See,' Longeye said, indicating in the middle distance a group of fallen trees. 'The Yankees have found a good place to fight.'

'They can't be carrying much food,' Moosejaw replied. 'We can wait them out. Let hunger and cold do our work.'

Longeye looked up to the sky. The heavy snow clouds were edging ever nearer. 'And what about Bearpaw?' he said. 'Will we let him starve too?' He rose to his feet. 'Wait here,' he said. 'I will be back soon.'

★   ★   ★

Kitty stood by the doorway to the cabin. She held the cast-iron skillet two-handed at head height like a housewife about to beat a dusty carpet. Her heart pounded as she waited for Jacques Marat to return. Presently she heard him approaching from his wigwam. He was singing in a raucous voice, '*Jolie blond, jolie fille, t'es partie, oui pour longtemps . . .*'

The song stopped as Marat reached the door. 'Are you ready, *mam'selle*, to welcome your charming guest?' he called.

Kitty Persimmon took a deep breath and steadied herself. '*Mais oui, monsieur,*' she called back.

The door was pushed open and Marat, a bottle of brandy in his hand, stepped inside, a broad and horrible leer upon his dingy countenance. As his front foot crossed the threshold Kitty swung the skillet with all her power.

The flat base of the pan caught the outlaw full in the face, crushing his nose and sending him reeling backwards. The young woman stepped after him and swung the pan again, backhanded and upwards. The blow struck Marat on the side of the jaw and sent him spinning to the ground. Blood was gushing from his nose. Kitty flung the skillet at him. Glancing around, she saw the outlaw's pony across the clearing. Lifting up her long skirts she ran to it. Behind her she heard the Metis growling and cursing as he struggled to regain his senses.

Kitty pulled herself up into the saddle of the pony and attempted to kick her mount into movement. The pinto, however, was only used to one rider — Marat. Feeling a stranger on his back made the animal nervous. He whinnied, stamped the ground and bucked. In desperation Kitty slapped him hard on the rump. With a great snort the pony took off at a gallop.

They had gone about forty yards

when Marat, collecting his wits bellowed out, 'Montcalm!'

Hearing his master call his name, the pony stopped abruptly. Kitty slid straight over his head, landing with a thump. In a moment she was back on her feet and running. The ground ahead was flat and open. She ran as quickly as her clothing would allow.

She had not gone far when she heard the sound of the pony's hoofs pounding the frozen turf. Glancing over her shoulder she saw that Marat was galloping in pursuit and closing fast. If she carried on along this route the outlaw would soon run her down; instead Kitty swerved off to her right and into a forest. The land here sloped sharply downwards. She plunged blindly through the pine and fir trees, breathlessly slipping, falling and rising again, only to trip once more. Behind her she could hear Marat breathing hard, yelling curses. Kitty had no idea how near he was and that only increased her desperation. The young woman was slithering between two pine trees, glancing back over her shoulder when she caught a toe under an exposed root and tumbled forward.

Trees and bushes clawed at her face, the sky appeared and disappeared as she rolled and somersaulted down the escarpment. After a few moments the tumbling stopped as she hit a patch of flat mossy ground. Kitty shook her head, trying to free herself of dizziness, and rose uncertainly to her feet. She had landed on a flat plateau twenty yards wide by fifteen deep. The plateau was bounded on two sides by sheer granite cliffs. On the third side the ground ended in a straight drop of some twenty-five feet, below which the dark, deep waters of a river rushed by. The only way out was the direction the young woman had come from and that avenue of escape was closed to her.

Kitty looked around for something to defend herself with. She found an oak branch the size and weight of a rolling pin, picked it up and waited for Marat. The young woman did not have to wait long. Soon the outlaw forced his way through the last of the trees and stood before her. His nose was still bleeding, the side of his face was swollen and his left eye had begun to close. He was hissing and swearing and brandishing a twelve-inch nick-bladed hunting knife in his right-hand.

'So the little lady likes to play dirty, huh?' He grimaced. 'Well, guess what? Old Jacques can play plenty dirty too.'

The outlaw began to approach her, body slightly crouched, shoulders swaying, head still, tossing the knife from hand to hand. Kitty instinctively backed away. Marat kept advancing, chuckling and snarling, outlining the foul acts he had planned for her, the steel blade flashing in his fists. When he was a few paces away he made a sudden leap at her. Startled, Kitty stumbled backwards and screamed as the ground suddenly disappeared from beneath her feet. For a moment she felt oddly weightless, then she was falling. She hit the freezing water feet first, and immediately disappeared beneath it, the chill kicking the breath from her lungs. Feeling the soles of her lace-up boots hit the riverbed, she kicked furiously, saw the light above grow brighter and then gasped in air as her head broke the surface.

Kitty was facing upstream. A few yards to her left a great fir tree was floating past. With a huge effort she spun on to her stomach and began to thrash the water. The trunk was not far away but swimming against the dragging weight of her voluminous clothing and with the current running across her, it seemed to Kitty as if she were swimming an ocean. Legs kicking, arms swinging, her lungs burning like they were on fire; she forced herself forward inch by inch, until finally she could reach out and grab the floating tree. She pulled herself alongside it, wrapped her right arm around the trunk and raised her chin above the water. From the cliff Marat roared out all the hideous things he wanted to do to her. Kitty was freezing cold, she had no idea where he was, or in what direction he was travelling. All she knew was that the river was carrying her away from the outlaw camp. For the moment that was enough.

9

From their position on the riverbank Morgan and Bishop continued to watch for Longeye and his men. As he waited Morgan once again noticed the military markings on the butt of the revolving rifle. He recalled the conversation he and the deputy US marshal had had at the widow's boarding house the night before they had set out on their mission — an event which now seemed a lifetime away.

Bishop had ridden with the Confederate bushwhackers of Bloody Bill Anderson and Archie Clement. Something in that puzzled Morgan. When the Civil War ended most of those men had become outlaws, like the Youngers and Frank and Jesse James. Bishop had chosen exactly the opposite course.

'So how is it that a man who served alongside Cole Younger is riding on the side of the law these days?' Morgan asked.

Bishop turned briefly to look at his comrade. 'Have you been cogitating on that for some while, Mr Morgan?' he asked. The former lawman admitted he had. There was a moment's silence, then Bishop spoke.

'Oddly enough, I was thinking on it myself just now. What brought it to mind is that Smith & Wesson pistol you carry — it was the model favoured by Jesse James, and maybe still is for all I know.'

There was a pause while Bishop vigilantly scanned the area in front of his position, then he continued, 'I am a man, Mr Morgan, who has born witness to the horrors that occur when law breaks down. I was there when Rocheport was razed to the ground, and at Centralia too, when it was sacked. When you take away the law what you are left with is human nature. And I have seen enough, Mr Morgan, not to place too much faith in that.'

Bishop once again took a moment to focus on the ground ahead of him, then went on, 'One night during the summer of 1864 we raided up into central Missouri. We hit a small town round about midnight. It was a beautiful Southern evening, a full moon, the air filled with the scent of honeysuckle and magnolia. I never knew the name of the place. We rode in roughshod and commenced shooting, burning, killing in the name of Dixie. After a while the pastor came running out from the little grey clapboard church they had. He was a short old man, chubby, with white hair ringed about his head. He was wearing his nightshirt. Gave the impression of an elderly choirboy.

'The pastor called out, 'You are devils! You are devils!' And young Archie Clement, he looked down at that old boy from that big black horse of his and he yelled right back, 'We are devils maybe, but we fight on the side of the angels.''

'And what did the pastor reply to

that?' Morgan asked quietly.

Bishop let out a bitter laugh. 'I don't know, Mr Morgan. It was hard to hear over the sound of Archie's revolver . . . '

A silence fell. When Bishop spoke again it was with far more urgency. 'Keep an eye out, Mr Morgan, we have visitors, approaching from the west.'

The band of four Lakotas swooped down fast. Riding with their heads low, hunting bows drawn, they yelped and whooped as they came on. Morgan and Bishop barely had time to alter their positions to cover the threat when arrows began thumping into the mud and timber around them. Morgan fired a couple of rounds at the nearest brave, but the suddenness of the attack and the speed and movement of the Indian ponies confused his aim and he missed both times. Bishop was more measured. His first shot tore a hole in the thigh of one of the Indians. By the time he had slotted another shell into the buffalo gun however, the Lakotas had whirled around and galloped away.

'Looks like they don't have much stomach for a fight,' Morgan said, as he reloaded his rifle with his cold and clumsy fingers.

Bishop shook his head. 'They were just probing,' he said. 'Seeing how many we are and what weapons we pack. Be assured, Mr Morgan, a Lakota has no greater pleasure in life than fighting.'

'You've encountered them before?' Morgan asked, finally clicking the cylinder back into the Remington rifle.

'A couple of times when recovering fugitives from justice in Indian territory,' Bishop said. 'The best I can say of the experience is that facing the Cheyenne is worse. Is there whiskey left in that flask, Mr Morgan?'

Morgan nodded and handed Bishop the flask. The deputy US marshal tilted back his head to drink, wincing slightly at the pain his cracked rib gave him. When he had taken his draught he nodded up at the sky.

'Those snow clouds are rolling our way. Normally I'd think getting caught in a blizzard in the mountains was something to be avoided, but here and now it's maybe the best chance we have.'

Morgan's brow furrowed. Mention of the impending storm reminded him that he needed to get Kitty back, and soon. Leaving his position he walked quickly over to the black gelding and began checking the saddle.

'What are you doing, Mr Morgan?' Bishop asked.

'To get Miss Persimmon,' Morgan replied, stowing the rifle in its scabbard, 'you said yourself that she must be with Marat. I've got a chance to find her before the blizzard hits, and I intend to use it.'

Reluctantly Bishop turned away from his position and walked over to the former lawman with a smile and placed a hand on his arm.

'In situations such as this, Mr Morgan,' he said, 'it never does for a man to allow sentiment to shade his judgement.'

'You can call it sentiment,' Morgan replied hotly, shaking the marshal's hand away. 'I call it values. I was raised to protect those I care about, not abandon them. You talk of upholding the law, Bishop. Well, there are two types of law. There's the law written on paper by politicians, and there's the law a man carries inside himself. That's the code I'm planning on upholding. If doing it kills me, then so be it. I intend to leave this world justified.'

Bishop shook his head, but the smile remained. 'Admirably put, Mr Morgan,' he said. 'But you miss my point. In your haste, you have overlooked something: you and I know that Bearpaw is dead, Louis Longeye does not. By now the outlaws will have realized that any direct assault on our position will end in carnage. If they want to kill us and free Bearpaw they will need to lure us out into the open. For that they need Miss Persimmon. They will bring her to us, Mr Morgan.'

Morgan knew straight away that the marshal was right, but he was too proud and angry to admit it.

'I suppose that's possible,' he mumbled.

The deputy US marshal reached out again and grabbed Morgan's arm. It was not a friendly gesture this time. His powerful fingers held the other man's wrist in a grip as powerful as a bench vice.

'Stop pouting, Mr Morgan,' he hissed in the steely tone he had last used when poking a revolver in the law student's belly. 'I don't ask you to admire my character, but by now you might at least give credit to my intelligence. Run off if you want to, though I can't guarantee a Christian burial if you do.' So saying, he released his grip, turned and walked back to his position.

Feeling humbled and slightly ashamed of himself Morgan drew the revolving rifle from its scabbard and followed him.

* * *

Marat roared and cursed at the yellow-haired girl until the river had carried her out of sight. Then he turned away and struggled back up the slope through the trees. His head throbbed worse than ever, his nose was busted and he couldn't see much of anything out of one eye. Worse, though, was the knowledge that he had let the woman escape. Louis would not be pleased when he found that out, not pleased at all. Marat turned things over in his mind as he wheezed his way up towards the outlaw camp. His best hope was that Louis had already killed the Clergyman and Crooked Hands and freed Billy. Then they could search for the woman together. She would have nowhere to go, no rescuer near by to save her. For a moment he brightened.

Then the memory of the men the Clergyman had killed in Lone Pine came back to him. He'd even gunned down the trio Louis had sent to bushwhack him in the hotel when his attention was fixed on the jail. It was like he had eyes in the back of his head. And Crooked Hands: maybe he couldn't fight so well, but he was brave. Marat recalled their encounter in the judge's house, the way the man had stared implacably at him along the barrel of his revolver. By the time Marat had returned to camp the bruised and battered outlaw was deeply depressed. His mood was not improved by the sound of an approaching horse.

★ ★ ★

Longeye had ridden fast back to camp. It was vital they got things finished before the blizzard hit. The snow would provide cover for his foe, cancelling out his advantage in numbers. Rounding a stand of cottonoaks he entered the level ground of the camp. Standing in the centre of it was the bloodied figure of Marat. Longeye slipped from his pony and strode across to him, noting the cuts and bumps and the forlorn look on his lieutenant's face. For a moment he thought that Crooked Hands might have been here.

'Who did this?' he demanded.

Marat held up both his hands. 'Now look, Louis,' he said, 'I'll tell you the truth, *ami*. But you got to promise . . . '
Longeye did not wait for him to finish. Seized by a sudden anger at the smell of whiskey and vomit that clung to Marat he stepped forward and slapped the man hard with the back of his hand. The blow landed with such force that Marat spun through 180 degrees before he hit the floor.

'Jeez,' he yelped as he pulled himself on to all fours. 'You think I ain't taken enough of a beating already, Louis?'

Longeye's answer was short and brutal. He delivered a powerful kick to Marat's ribs that flipped him over on to his back.

'What the hell . . . ' Marat yelled.

The outlaw's protest was cut short by Longeye, who placed the heel of his buckskin boot on his blood brother's throat and pressed slowly down on his windpipe.

'You disgrace yourself, Jacques,' he snarled, increasing the pressure as

Marat attempted to force his foot away, his face turning red from lack of oxygen. 'Crawling on your belly for whiskey and women, like a dog that fears his master.'

Marat's eyes were bulging now and filled with terror. Longeye stared down into them and then, finally, lifted his foot from the other's throat and stalked off to the cabin in which Kitty Persimmon had been incarcerated. Coughing and spluttering Marat rose to his feet and followed.

'You untied the woman?' Longeye asked when they were inside the cabin.

Marat shook his head violently, setting pain shuddering through his skull.

'No. Wasn't anything I wanted from her I couldn't get easier if she was trussed up.' He saw the nail on the wall with the severed leather thongs hanging from it.

'See,' Marat said, pointing to them. 'She must have cut herself loose on that nail there. Then she waited inside the door and hit me with the skillet. Broke my damn nose. I was drunk. Louis, I ain't saying I wasn't, but it was you tied her up and put her in here.'

The outlaw chief looked at him, fire flashing in his eyes. 'So it is my fault?' he asked.

Marat shrank back, waggling his hands. 'I am not saying that, *mon frère*. Absolutely no. What I'm saying is — '

Whatever Marat had to say Longeye was not interested in it. 'Where is she?' he asked.

'Ran away down through the forest and fell in the river,' Marat replied. 'Last I saw she was floating downstream.'

Longeye turned and walked out of the hut. Marat trailed behind him.

'So what you plan? You killed the Clergyman yet?' he asked. The outlaw leader did not reply. He trotted across the camp ground, mounted his pony and set off to the east. Marat did likewise. Soon the two men were riding abreast of each other. After they had travelled a couple of miles Longeye turned his pony to the right and began to picking his way down through the trees.

'You figuring to fish her out, *ami?*' Marat asked.

Longeye ignored him, steering his mount between pines and firs until he came to the edge of the river. Here the water flowed slowly in a wide arc and the bank was shallow and edged with sand and stones. Without pausing the outlaw chief trotted his pony out into the river, and turned to look upstream.

★   ★   ★

Kitty Persimmon had been drifting on the river for twenty minutes. The young woman had no idea how far she had travelled. It could not have been more than a mile or two. She shivered uncontrollably and her teeth chattered. Her legs and feet were numb with cold. She had to leave the water soon or she would die in it. Even should she get back on to dry land her predicament was grave. Her heavy woollen dress and her cotton petticoats were soaked through. She had lost a boot when she fell in the river. She had no cloak or coat, no food and no means with which to make a fire.

A person in such a situation might easily have given in to despair. Kitty, though, was a woman of strong resolve. Her own mother had died giving birth to her and she had been raised by her father. The judge was a man who believed in the importance of remaining positive in all situations. Kitty shared that philosophy. In her present circumstance she could count three things for which she could truly be thankful: she was alive, she had escaped from Marat and somewhere out here in the wilderness she felt certain Isaac Morgan was searching for her.

The thought of Morgan brought a smile to her lips. She recalled the last time he'd visited her father, standing bashfully in the hallway, wringing his hat in his hands and jesting about the

Watsons. He'd shown another side of his nature the night she was kidnapped, facing down Marat with that pistol in his poor twisted fingers. Isaac would not let her down. She just had to hang on until he found her.

The river, she noticed now, had begun to widen. That must mean it was growing shallower too. When the tree she was clinging to stopped moving forwards — a branch caught on the riverbed — and began a slow counter-clockwise circle, Kitty decided that it was time to strike out for the shore. As the trunk turned broadside to the current she pulled herself along it hand over hand. Soon she was no more than twenty yards from the bank. Reluctantly relinquishing hold of her makeshift life raft Kitty began furiously propelling herself towards the shore.

Kicking and flailing, the weighty material of her clothing dragging her in every direction but the one in which she wanted to go, Kitty battled across the water. After a struggle that expended almost all the strength she had left the young woman felt her feet striking the hard surface of the riverbed. With one final effort she raised herself upright and waded the last few yards to land. Staggering exhausted, she collapsed on her back on the shale beach, chest heaving. Looking up she saw through the haze of tiredness that the sky was menacingly dark. A blizzard was coming. She closed her eyes for a moment, trying to work through a list of what she must do next.

When she opened them again she saw something even more unwelcome than the banks of snow clouds: the face of Louis Longeye.

The Metis leader poked the yellow-haired woman a couple of times in the ribs with the toe of his boot, then grabbed her wrists, hauled her to her feet and in one unbroken movement threw her over one powerful shoulder.

'You move, I cut your throat,' he told her. There was neither anger nor cruelty in his voice, but Kitty had no doubt he meant exactly what he said.

Longeye carried the woman to his pony. As he tossed Kitty across its back she caught sight of the legs of another pony standing alongside. Then she heard a familiar voice say,

'Pleasure to see you again, *mam'-selle*. Lookin' forward to renewing our acquaintance.'

Longeye and Marat rode back across the river, the water splashing up into Kitty's face from the hoofs of the ponies. They rode up the wooded slope on the other side until they hit flat grassland. Here they urged their mounts onwards and were soon travelling fast across the frozen ground.

*   *   *

Bishop had cleaned, oiled and reloaded all his weapons. He'd taken the Colt Peacemaker from the gunbelt of the unfortunate Watson and inspected that too, before shoving the burnished steel pistol into the top of his left boot. He was inspecting the Hawken flintlock musket that Morgan had taken from the body of Henri Youngbuck, sighting down the long barrel and remarking that the gun had been the finest hunting weapon in North America until 'Old Christian Sharps set up shop in Philadelphia'. When a mournful bird call sounded in the still air of the late afternoon, once, twice and then a third time, Bishop cocked his head.

'You hear that?' he asked Morgan.

The other man nodded. 'Whippoor-will,' he replied. 'Back East where I was raised they say he only calls when he senses a soul about to depart the body. Guess that's about right for the current situation, though it's kind of early in the evening to be hearing one.'

Bishop scratched his chin. 'It's late in the year too, Mr Morgan. Whippoor-wills fly south in September. That's Longeye calling in his troops. The parlay is coming. We better make preparations.'

With Bishop's help Morgan inserted the Hawken rifle up the back of Plug

Watson's coat and tucked the barrel under the dead boy's gunbelt. When seated on a horse, the body of the unfortunate young deputy would remain upright. Together they lifted the corpse into the saddle of Betsy and tied rope around the horse furniture to secure it.

Ten minutes later Moosejaw rode out from the treeline brandishing a white flag on the end of a cottonwood branch. Bishop mounted on Samson went out to meet him. He returned a few minutes later.

'We're to ride out with 'Bearpaw.' They'll do the same with Miss Persimmon. 'We meet them midway between the trees and the river. We give them Longeye's nephew, they give us the captive and then we all ride away whistling a happy tune. Or so they say.'

'Except we don't have Bearpaw,' Morgan said grimly.

'Even if we had, Mr Morgan,' Bishop replied, 'I don't believe it would make the slightest difference. Longeye has no intention of leaving us alive, or returning Miss Persimmon to her father.'

'Do you have a plan to stop him?' Morgan asked.

Bishop scratched his chin. 'None that I invest total faith in, no,' he replied with a faint smile.

'You care to share the least bad option, then?' Morgan asked.

10

Five minutes later the two men left the relative safety of their riverbank stockade. Morgan rode on the left, Bishop on the right. The rigid body of Plug Watson was between them, strapped tightly to the stocky bulk of his father's mare.

As they advanced towards the trees they saw the outlaw party riding slowly towards them. Longeye and Moosejaw were in the centre, flanked on either side by a cluster of three Lakota braves. Kitty Persimmon was on foot, stumbling ahead of the two mounted Metis. It was the first time Morgan had seen her since the night Marat dragged her from the judge's porch. To his relief she appeared unharmed.

'Marat isn't with them,' Bishop said quietly. 'My guess is he's somewhere along the edge of that wood, drawing a bead on one of us. You had best hold that in mind, Mr Morgan, when the gunplay starts.'

The two parties continued their slow, suspicious progress towards one another. When there was no more than twenty paces between them Bishop reined in Samson and held out his arm for Morgan to do the same. Longeye and his men halted too. For a moment the two groups stared at one another through the rising steam of their own and their horses' breath. The air was unnaturally still, as it often is before a storm, and the day was so quiet that Morgan felt sure he could hear the blood pumping fast through his veins. As he looked across at Kitty and her captors he felt something cold land on his cheek. Glancing quickly upwards saw the first flakes of snow falling from the darkening sky.

Bishop must have noticed the snow too because at that moment he took a deep breath and barked,

'Let's go to it, Mr Morgan.'

Morgan reacted fast, reaching down

to his right and pulling the sawed-off shotgun from its concealment in Watson's left boot. Yelling for Kitty to hit the ground, he did as Bishop had instructed, aiming the weapon low at the legs of the outlaws' ponies. At twenty paces the sawn-off was hardly life threatening, but its short barrel gave a wide spread ten yards across. When the gun roared it sent small beads of stinging metal into the knees and cannons of the outlaws' mounts. The ponies reared and bucked in pain and fear.

Tossing the shotgun aside, Morgan drew his six-shooter and urged Beau forwards. In an instant the judge's faithful old horse was standing right above Kitty who was lying face down on the grass. Morgan called out to her urgently and, recognizing his voice, the young woman rose quickly to her feet. Looking up at him she gave him a smile that hit him straight in the chest. Feeling renewed hope, Morgan reached down and pulled her on to the rear of his horse.

To his left he saw that one of the Lakotas had already brought his mount under control and was now charging towards them. The warrior had a stone-headed club raised in his right hand, and was holding the reins of his pony between snarling teeth. Morgan fired twice. The second shot hit the brave in the shoulder and sent him spinning to the ground.

While this had been going on Bishop had drawn his Remington with the intention of bringing an end to Louis Longeye. The outlaw had thwarted him, however. Slipping nimbly from his bucking horse the minute the first shot was fired, he was how using the whirling, frightened pony for cover. Unable to get a clean shot at the Metis, Bishop instead pumped two rounds into the body of Moosejaw, who fell to the ground in a writhing heap.

Turning Samson to his right Bishop fired his remaining four rounds into the Lakotas, killing one and sending the other two riding for cover. As they galloped away, the deputy US marshal calmly holstered his pistol, drew the Winchester and with the unhurried air of a man shooting crows in his backyard, dropped both of them. As the last brave fell screaming to the ground, Bishop turned back to the left and again searched the battle site for Longeye. The Metis, though, had disappeared into thin air amongst the quivering, bucking mass of terrified, riderless ponies. Once again the huge outlaw's ability to make himself invisible astounded the marshal.

The snow was falling hard now, big heavy flakes dimming the light and blurring the vision. Bishop picked out Morgan thirty yards away with what looked to be the young woman on the back of his horse. They were galloping in the direction of the river, the two remaining Lakotas bearing down on them from behind, war clubs held high. Spinning in the saddle Morgan raised his revolver to fire, but before he could squeeze the trigger a shot rang out from the tree line. Marat. The musket ball struck the ex-lawman's arm. He dropped his weapon and cried out in pain.

Bishop urged Samson forward and fired the Winchester one-handed at the Indians as they closed on his wounded comrade. His first shot hit one of them squarely enough in the side to knock him from his pony, but the other galloped on and was soon hidden from the marshal's sight by Morgan and Kitty. Not daring to risk another shot, the lawman dug his spurs into Samson's flanks and, bent low over the stallion's neck, raced towards the mêlée.

Marat's musketball had shattered a bone in Morgan's forearm. The pain was agonizing and the limb hung limp and useless by his side. The former lawman had little time to dwell on his predicament, however. The two braves were bearing down on them. Old Beau had never been the fastest horse, and with two people on his back he was moving as if through heavy clay. The Lakotas' agile ponies gained on him with every stride.

'Reach into the right saddle-bag and take the gun,' Morgan said over his shoulder. Kitty did as instructed. Unbuckling the leather strap and reaching inside she pulled out the pepperbox pistol.

'It's loaded,' Morgan gasped, the pain shooting through his arm as Beau jolted and bumped over the hard, snowy ground. 'Put it in your pocket and only fire it when you're close to the target.' Kitty glanced quickly at the little gun, then shoved it into the side pocket of her dress. As she did so she heard a rifle crack from her left rear, and looking back saw one of the pursuing warriors tumble from his pony.

The death of his compatriot seemed to spur the other brave onwards. A few seconds later he was galloping alongside them. Switching his war club from his right to his left hand the Indian began swinging it at Morgan, who attempted to avoid the blows by turning Beau away to the left.

The Lakota was not so easily dislodged. His pony was fast and lithe and, like all of his tribe, he had learned to ride almost as soon as he could stand. Steering the horse using his knees, he continued to swing the stone-headed club at the wounded Morgan, who swayed and dodged as best he could. Hanging on behind him, Kitty thought of using her newly acquired pistol against the brave, but the constant swerving and bouncing meant that it was all she could do to stay on the horse, her arms closed tight around Morgan's waist.

Bishop was riding hard in pursuit of friend and foe. He had the reins in his left hand and was using the crook of that arm as a rest for the Winchester. The swirling snow and the constant movement of the horses were preventing him lining up a clear shot.

With Kitty clinging hard to him Morgan continued to duck and swing away from his adversary's increasingly frenzied blows. Several struck him, but glanced off, bruising his upper arm and shoulder. As another swing of the club missed his face by a fraction of an inch, he heard the voice of Bishop bellowing from somewhere to his left rear.

'Turn to the right, Mr Morgan. Turn to the right!' Noting that even in these desperate moments the marshal still persisted in using his title, Morgan did as instructed, pulling sharply on the reins of Beau.

As the burly black horse turned, the Lakota's pony slapped right into him and for a moment Morgan and the warrior were shoulder to shoulder, staring straight into each other's eyes. Then two shots rang out and the warrior was gone.

Morgan looked around and saw that he and Kitty were no longer being pursued. He allowed Beau to drop from a gallop to a canter and then to a trot. The stout-hearted old horse was huffing and puffing and sweat rolled down his shoulders and chest, freezing on his dark hide the moment it cooled.

Bishop came alongside. 'Are you in good health, Miss Persimmon?' he asked.

The young woman replied that she was, 'And feeling better by the moment,' she added.

'And you, Mr Morgan,' Bishop asked. The ex-lawman indicated his shattered arm. 'Marat,' he said. 'One of the bones is broken, but there doesn't seem to be any blood.'

Bishop bent forward to look at Morgan's sleeve. 'The ball doesn't seem even to have penetrated through the canvas and sheepskin of your coat,' he said. 'Still, you'll need to get to a doctor as fast as you can, or risk losing the arm. Do you think you can find your way to Lone Pine in these conditions?'

'Why?' Morgan asked in surprise. 'Where are you going?'

Bishop, who had started to turn his horse around, looked at him sternly.

'To get Longeye,' he said.

Morgan reached out with his left hand and grabbed the marshal's arm.

'Wait a moment,' he said. 'Are you crazy? You'll never find him in this blizzard, and even if you do you'll likely freeze to death afterwards.'

'It's a gamble, I admit,' the deputy US marshal responded. 'But a pot this big is rarely on the table, Mr Morgan. If I fold now I may regret it for ever.' Shaking loose the other man's grip, he dug his spurs into Samson's flanks and was soon swallowed up by the blizzard.

Kitty fixed Morgan's broken arm in a sling. The snowstorm still raged, but the wounded man's trappings included a compass from his army days. Using that instrument to navigate through the swirling whiteness they began the slow journey back to Lone Pine. After an hour the snow began to ease. A quarter of an hour later it had stopped altogether. They halted to dust the pale powder from their coats and saddles and from the backs of the horses. Morgan broke out the beef jerky and biscuits he'd provisioned himself with. The last of the judge's heart-warming bourbon was drunk.

Morgan surveyed the pale landscape; the snow had fallen heavily and drifted in the wind, burying all trace of the recent battles.

'I guess at some point, when the weather has eased, we'll have to ride out here with Sheriff Watson and try and recover the body of his son,' he said. 'Though if Longeye is still on the loose, attracting volunteers for that task won't exactly be easy. I can't say I much want to see him again myself. I hope Bishop found him.'

* * *

When the shooting started Longeye had slipped from his pony and used the horses as cover. He'd darted from one to another, all the while keeping his eye on the Clergyman. By now he had a deep respect for this particular Yankee's gunplay. Flitting between the bucking and rearing horses he made his way towards his nephew. Bearpaw's horse, too, was shying and leaping with panic, but the young man held on firmly. It was only when Longeye got closer that he realized the young man in the saddle was not his nephew. And that whoever this man was, he was dead.

The snow had begun to fall. Soon it had blotted out everything that was more than ten feet away. Disoriented and puzzled by what he had discovered, Longeye blundered off in what he hoped was the direction of the trees.

★   ★   ★

Marat had shot Crooked Hands and then reloaded his gun with the intention of putting a bullet in the Clergyman. By the time he was through with tamping down the wadding into the muzzle-loader, however, the snow had begun, obliterating his view of the skirmish. The woodsman had quickly found a wide-spreading birch tree. He had spread a buffalo robe over the lower branches to make a shelter and was tucked underneath it. His nose throbbed. He wondered if Longeye had killed the Yankees and rescued Bearpaw.

He hoped he had recaptured the yellow-haired woman. He had plans for her. Nice plans.

From somewhere deep within the blizzard Marat heard a bird call, once, twice, three times. Louis Longeye. He mimicked it: '*Whip-poor-will.*' The call and response was repeated several times before Marat saw the dark outline of a man emerging from the snowstorm. He stood up to greet his old friend.

'Are the Yankees dead, *ami?*' He asked.

'I'm afraid not, *monsieur,*' said a voice he did not recognize. A pistol muzzle flashed three times in the murky light. The slugs from Bishop's revolver hit Marat in the chest. The Metis stumbled backwards into the birch. He would have fallen but the tree branches held him upright.

'You are not the bird I expected, Yankee,' he snarled, then he returned fire, the Hawken rifle held at his hip. The flintlock roared, spitting fire from its barrel. The ball flew through the whirling snowflakes and struck the marshal in the left-shoulder. Barely pausing, the lawman fired three more shots into Marat, ending his life.

Bishop touched his hand to his wound. It came back red with blood. He walked back to Samson and with an effort pulled himself into the saddle. He waited a moment, making certain of his bearings, then rode off to the east. The pain in his shoulder jolted into his brain with every step the horse took. He could feel the fresh blood trickling down his arm. He felt faint and sick. The snow was blinding him and images of the Civil War started popping into his mind. Things he had forgotten, or had tried to forget.

*   *   *

Longeye heard the pistol shots from somewhere behind him, then the hunting rifle fired, then came more pistol shots. He knew what it must mean. The Clergyman had found Marat. The outlaw stared up at the sky, feeling the cold, damp snow landing on his face. His people had fallen like the snow, till their bodies covered the ground.

Longeye was tired, but he knew that if he lay down he would die. Instead he forced himself to keep on moving and to think. Bearpaw had not been with the Yankees. They had brought a corpse dressed in his clothes. Once again the whitemen had deceived him. Bearpaw must still be in the jail. All the rest of the gang were dead now. There was only Billy left. If he could get there before the Clergyman he could free him.

Longeye plunged through the snow. Every once in a while he stopped to check for moss on the bark of the trees, so that he knew he was heading south-eastwards. He marched on remorselessly, the snow gradually rising from his ankles to his calves. It had reached his knees when at last it stopped.

Longeye paused now and listened. Somewhere to his right he heard a man and woman talking. Crooked Hands and the yellow-haired woman. They were coming towards him. Longeye glanced around and saw that the westerly wind had blown the snow into a deep drift against a stand of low pine trees. He ran across to it and began digging, using his huge hands like shovels.

★   ★   ★

Bishop had ridden slowly after dispatching Marat. Blood still trickled from the wound in his shoulder. He had hoped it would stop naturally. When it didn't he dismounted under some tall Douglas firs and fashioned a compress from cloth and moss scraped from bark, which would at least temporarily stanch the flow. Once he was bandaged he pulled himself back on to the big chestnut stallion with a grunt of effort and set off again. The blizzard continued. He drifted into a half-sleep, thinking of Archie Clement, Cole Younger and Frank James, picturing all the men he had killed. Somewhere in the swirling, silent blankness Louis Longeye was waiting for him. One of them must die, that was certain.

The deputy US marshal rode on through the deepening snow. The world had become a shadowy landscape in which everything was black-and-white. Every so often Bishop was jolted out of his fitful state by the sight of what he was certain was the looming figure of the outlaw chief, only to discover as he got closer that what had looked like the outline of a man was simply a snow-covered tree or bush.

The snow stopped after a couple of hours, the clouds rolled away and the sun appeared low in the sky to the west. The fresh powdered land shimmered in the light and Bishop pulled his hat brim lower to shield his eyes from the glare. He had just surmounted the crest of a low rise when he caught sight of Morgan and Kitty Persimmon half a mile to the east. They were walking. Kitty was leading Beau. The old gelding was a steady type but his sound character was not matched by his stamina. Walking in deep drifts was a drain on the energy of any creature. The veteran horse was in need of a rest.

The deputy US marshal was riding towards the couple when suddenly a patch of snow immediately to their left seemed to explode and a dark creature emerged in a cloud of powder. For a brief instant Bishop thought it was the scavenging wolverine, then the creature let out a war whoop and he realized it was something even more dangerous than that.

* * *

Morgan and Kitty were trudging through the snow enjoying the warmth of the afternoon sun reflecting from the whitened ground. Morgan's shattered arm throbbed, but every smile Kitty gave him eased the pain. They had just passed a cluster of small pine trees where the snow had drifted into deep piles when they heard the war cry of the Metis chief. Longeye had dug out a pit in the snowdrift and, crouching in it, was completely concealed from view. Now he sprang from his hiding place and bounded over the snow towards them, his black and white painted face contorted with malice.

Kitty shrieked as she saw him and Morgan reached with his left arm to cross-draw the Smith & Wesson from his holster. As he withdrew the revolver the hammer got momentarily caught in the sling and he tugged it free so wildly that his first shot went straight into the air. By the time he'd got the gun under control again the giant outlaw was only ten yards away. Morgan levelled the pistol unsteadily, but once again Longeye astounded him with his agility. The Metis sidestepped as he ran, so that in the space of a few strides he had come up behind Kitty. Before the former lawman could properly comprehend what was happening the young woman let out a yell of pain and terror as Longeye grabbed her arm. Spinning her round he grasped her from behind. One of his huge hands gripped her chin, the other pinned her throat.

'Drop your gun or I break her neck,' he snarled.

Morgan did not doubt he meant it. Raising his left hand out to his side he reluctantly dropped the Smith & Wesson into the snow.

'What do you want, Longeye?' he asked.

Longeye began to back away from Morgan towards old Beau. 'I want Billy freed from jail.' he said, 'You were supposed to bring him to me, but you brought a dead man instead.'

Morgan felt a lurch in his belly. Replying as evenly as he could, the former lawman spoke,

'Bearpaw? Sure, I can arrange that. In return for the woman.' Longeye stared hard at him. Something in the Yankee's voice and face was not right. His pale eyes shifted away when he spoke.

'You lie, Crooked Hands,' he growled. 'Where is Billy?' As he awaited the reply he stepped back until he could feel the bulk of the black horse directly behind him.

As Morgan watched, sickness rising in his stomach, he noticed Kitty's hand slipping into the pocket of her dress.

'What do you mean, Longeye?' he said. 'We left Billy in the jail.'

Kitty's hand emerged, clutching the little pepperbox pistol. Slowly and naturally she let the hand holding the gun drop back down to her side. When it bumped against Longeye's leg just above the knee Kitty pulled the trigger. Six barrels of .70 lead raked into the outlaw's knee, down his shin and into the top of his foot, shredding the skin and breaking bone as they did so. With a yell of surprise and pain the outlaw released his grip on the young woman. Elbowing her captor in the ribs Kitty broke free and ran towards Morgan. The outlaw tried to pursue, but his bloody right leg buckled under him and he tumbled face first into the snow.

Morgan quickly retrieved his revolver

and pointed the gun at the prone figure.

'You stay right where you are,' he shouted. 'Don't even think about getting up.'

The sound of a galloping horse caused Morgan to spin in his tracks. Expecting to see a war-painted Lakota he laughed in relief when he realized it was Bishop.

'Marshal,' he called out with a smile. 'Glad you could make it.'

The deputy US marshal did not respond. It was if he had not heard. His eyes were focused on Longeye, his face was pale. He dismounted from his horse, brushed past Morgan and Kitty and strode over to the outlaw, drawing his revolver as he did so. When he arrived at the prone form of the giant Metis, Bishop stamped his right boot down on to the man's spine and pointed the pistol at the back of his head.

'What are you doing?' Morgan asked in disbelief. Bishop's only response was to pull back the hammer on the revolver. 'Hold up, Marshal,' Morgan called urgently.

'Remember what you said to me this afternoon? Executing a man in cold blood — how is that belief in the law?'

Bishop slowly turned to look at his questioner. He indicated the bloody wound at his shoulder.

'Don't have time to wait on Judgement Day,' he said, in tones Morgan barely recognized. The Southern accent was stronger and the voice seemed to come from somewhere far away in place and time. There was an expression on the marshal's face such as Morgan had not seen before, either. The lawman's eyes were blank and sunken. His cheeks were drawn, his skin chalky. Morgan realized with a jolt that this was how Bishop must have appeared to the citizens of Centralia and Rocheportt and on the night in Missouri when Archie Clement shot the white-haired pastor.

'You don't have to do this, Marshal,' Morgan said. Bishop stared at him as if at a total stranger.

'Hush your mouth, boy,' he drawled, his voice twisted with brutality, 'and cover the lady's ears.'

Morgan did not argue. He did as he was told. When the marshal saw that his instructions had been followed he turned his gaze back to the prone figure of Louis Longeye and pulled the trigger. The outlaw's body bucked as the slug struck him between the shoulder blades. Bishop fired again, and again and again. Even when the last bullet was spent and the hammer struck home with nothing more than a metallic click he went on firing.

Morgan had watched the scene with horror. Now he softly called out the marshal's name. At first Bishop did not seem to hear him, then he took a deep breath and with what appeared to be a huge effort shook his head like a man trying to free himself of a vivid nightmare. He took his foot off the corpse of Louis Longeye and, turning his back to Morgan and Kitty, began slowly and methodically reloading the Remington.

When he turned to face them again he was wearing his characteristic placid yet watchful expression.

'I am grateful for the assistance you afforded me, Mr Morgan,' he said in his usual even, polite tones. 'I wish both you and Miss Persimmon well.' He touched the brim of his Mosby hat, bowed slightly to Kitty, nodded to Morgan, then walked across and mounted his horse.

'What about that bullet wound?' Kitty called after him. 'It needs dressing.'

Bishop did not reply. Without once glancing back he urged the big stallion into a trot and rode away.

'He'll bleed to death out there,' Kitty said.

Morgan's eyes followed Deputy US Marshal Bishop, 'I wouldn't bet on it,' he said.

For a while Morgan and Kitty watched Bishop disappearing eastwards across the snowy land, then the young woman shivered slightly and, looking up at Morgan with a smile, said, 'Isaac, will you take me home?'

Several hours later they rode into Lone Pine. Main Street was deserted.

The heavy snowfall had driven the inhabitants indoors. From The Dutchman's saloon came the sound of a piano. Frenchy was playing *Turkey in the Straw*. It was a little after 7 p.m. At the bottom of the street the lamps were lit in the Persimmon house and pale grey woodsmoke curled upward from the chimneys.

DRY GULCH REVENGE

Clay More

Hank Hawkins has the opportunity to achieve his ambition of buying a ranch. All he has to do is help a gang rob the stage in the Devil's Bones canyons. But it turns out the bandits never intended to leave anyone alive — including him . . . Upon regaining consciousness, Hawkins vows to track down the murderers who betrayed him. But when he sets off, he has a companion accompanying him: Helen Curtis, the fiancee of the messenger whose death lies heavy on Hawkins' conscience.

THE OUTLAWS OF SALTY'S NOTCH

Fenton Sadler

The elderly derelicts in the sleepy Louisiana settlement of La Belle Commune are leading the good life, lazing in the hot sun — until Bushwhack Jack Breaker rides in from Texas with his outlaw band. Former bounty hunter Paladin awakes to find that Marshal Brad Corrigan has been kidnapped, along with saloonist Rik Paulson and storekeeper Alec Mackie — but why? The elegant widow Emma Bowman-Laing knows where — but a rescue bid fails, and her crumbling mansion goes up in flames . . .